FLAT WHITE

ALSO BY BOB TRULUCK

Street Level (2000)
Saw Red (2003)
The Art of Redemption (2007)

FLAT WHITE

BOB TRULUCK

Flat White by Robert O. Truluck,

ISBN: 0990805301
ISBN-13: 978-0990805304

MURMUR HOUSE PRESS

MurmurHousePress.com

This book is dedicated to the roughly eight hundred thousand individuals incarcerated every year for non-violent cannabis infractions, the majority for simple possession. With 5% of the world's population and 25% of the world's prisoners, we've rendered ourselves nothing short of a prison state. We're ruining our young people's lives en masse with this prison-state culture and prison-for-profit mindset that we don't even remember creating. This is cannabis prohibition. This is why it must end.

Prohibition has made nothing but trouble.
Al Capone

For every prohibition you create, you also create an underground.
Jello Biafra

Prohibition didn't work in the Garden of Eden. Adam ate the apple.
Vicente Fox

Even if one takes every reefer madness allegation of the prohibitionists at face value, marijuana prohibition has done far more harm to far more people than marijuana ever could.
William F. Buckley, Jr.

When a man's partner is killed he's supposed to do something about it. It doesn't make any difference what you thought of him. He was your partner and you're supposed to do something about it.
Sam Spade/Dashiell Hammett

Roses

By Steven Foxbury

Who's that ghost there with the gun
He was the most amazing man
I'm appalled
I should stay but I think I'll go
Way up north from down below
Heard there's a town where I belong

And on my tombstone you can write down the words
Roses will never grow here
And on my tombstone you can write down the words
Roses will never grow here

Sure I'm poisoned down inside
Produced by soured swallowed pride
Took too many on the chin
Should've spoke when I shut up
I stood still when I had enough
Now even in my dreams I'm weak

And on my tombstone you can write down the words
Roses will never grow here
And on my tombstone you can write down the words
Roses will never grow here

I won't be the one with all of the answers when they call
for an explanation
I'll be wide-eyed and open mouthed
Spinning wheels to get words out
And disappointed when they don't

And on my tombstone you can write down the words
Roses will never grow here
And on my tombstone you can write down the words
Roses will never grow here

[1]

Maybe halfway through my second cup a county cop I know named Booker called, asked did I want to go look at a dead girl in the trunk of a car. I said *yeah* but I didn't really mean it.

The cop part of Booker read the insincere part of me, said I needed to ease his way, was something we needed to straighten out. I was thinking it was about a couple, three PRs involved in a case I was involved in a while back. These boys had insisted on letting their pursuit of the thug life get them in a permanently horizontal position. I'd absolved my sin in the matter down to venial self-defense and hadn't worried the proper authorities with the details. I figured some damning evidence had caught up with me and now Booker wanted to grill me about it. I was way wide on the Rickies, way wide.

Booker says, "I can see you on the fence bout whe'er to head my way or not, so let me help you out, Sloan. They was a cell phone stuck down in the seat a this car." Timed a little pause nicely, did: "You know the battery was dead but this cute little girl work for EMT say she got a charger for it I need it. See, she got a phone just like it for personal use."

We paused to see was I keeping up.

Seemed to be—my adrenals were humming like a motherfucker.

Booker noticed I didn't have anything to add, took it on. "I get the phone fired up—this little EMT tech helpin me—guess whose number comes up, last dial, name on the ID. Guess, Sloan."

I wouldn't guess. Didn't need to.

"Was you, Sloan. Had your name: *Duncan Sloan.*"

"What's that make me, a murderer?"

"Who say she murdered?"

I rebounded poorly with: "So what's that make me?"

"Make you involved, motherfucker. Might make you accessory, which is how I'm leanin right this minute. What me and you need to hash out, is it before or after the fact." Booker still pitching in his slow Southern style but peppering them up a bit.

"Come on, Booker. You know I didn't kill anybody."

"Lately maybe you didn't. Get your ass down here like while ago. And, Sloan, you need to leave the bullshit at the house."

[2]

The hookup with Booker was a clump of scrub, maybe three acres, where Edgewater becomes Bunnell and slips under the Orange Blossom Trail without many people noticing. Time I got there, there was already lots of yellow plastic tape and county employees doing stuff with cameras and other gadgets. Lots of rubber gloves and plastic bags. Center stage was a beat GM sled with an awful yellow paint job.

Stood off to one side, didn't see Booker. Scratched nut and acted like a curious yokel. Still no Booker.

I was ready to slide when Booker appeared, slid in beside me, moving with that quiet and graceful stealth God often assigns fat men. He said: "Glad you could make it. Let's see do you know 'er."

Booker nodded and tossed a cordiality here and there as we ducked under the yellow tape and walked to the rear of the car. He pulled a hand from a pocket. It clamped an official looking evidence bag; a small cell phone was in the bag. Neither phone nor bag got mentioned.

The girl was curled up on her side and most of her tongue poked out of her mouth. It was long and yellow and dehydrated. It reminded me of a plantain chip. The girl didn't care a damn what I thought—she was two good weeks past caring about anything.

Not in bad shape, though, for being in the trunk of a car for a while—given the climate here—but if she wasn't packing ID saying who she was then it was going to take the county boys with the gadgets to tell.

I was standing next to Booker, both of us arms folded and serious as a couple of Sadducees, and I thought about how the whole scene, particularly the plantain part, should probably be making me sick, but it wasn't. How it should be ruining my appetite, but wasn't. How there was a decently authentic Mex joint around the corner did nice things with *huevos.* One thought led to another until I heard myself saying, "Buy you some breakfast?"

"What? This shit makin you hongry?"

I thought about it, thought about how I got from the dead girl to the plantain chip to asking about breakfast. "Indirectly, I guess."

I was still looking at the girl but I could tell Booker was looking at me. "It don't bother you gettin caught with your pants down like this? Don't embarrass you or nothin?"

I shrugged out some dunno. What am I gonna say?

I said: "Breakfast or no?"

"You call that little pervert lawyer a yours?"

"Left a message."

"You feel the need for legal representation in this deal?" Being the cop now.

"I figure I retain Paulie Mopes and he hires me to investigate my problem..." I trailed it off, turned a couple of innocent palms up.

"What you sayin is you think you'd be entitled to some kinda client-attorney, attorney-investigator double-dip privilege."

I shrugged, nodded in accordance with how sure I was—wasn't much of a nod.

"You think it'll work? Seem awful complex for you and Mopes. Sure does, now."

Paulie may be a pervert and damn near a midget but he pulls off some amazing shit for a guy with a correspondence school education. I said, "Paulie's coin operated. I pay him, he'll make it happen."

Booker mmm-hmmed me some, said, "Little motherfucker remind me a the policy man used to visit my gran'mamma. This girl killed before or after you got the call?"

"Before."

Booker jerked a thumb at the girl as he turned. "You know 'er?" His tone didn't hold much hope.

"Doesn't look much like anybody I know." I turned and followed.

Booker stopped, put a cop face on me. "You sure?"

I gave some face back. "Booker, I might do some fucked-up shit once in a while, but if I knew who that girl was I'd tell you so you could tell her people."

Booker conceded with a semi-shrug. "I'll accept that."

I thanked him.

Walking to our cars, Booker said, "I b'lieve I'll pass on that breakfast. My blood sugar givin me a fit right now."

Stalled me a bit. Three hundred pound cops passing on free food? I let it go—Booker goes into fear for his retirement when I show up and I don't blame him. He's uncomfortable with my relaxed sense of obligation toward legal propriety. He also knows I don't swing on good guys, so he tolerates me. But I scare the shit out of him—him and those two lots on Cay Brac where he and the missus are planning on building the coquina house with attached tiki bar. I said, "Don't fuck around and die on us here before you get to retire, dad."

I got a grunt that didn't translate to anything. Then I got: "Who was it called you, Sloan?"

We walked. I said: "A friend. An old friend. What if it wasn't him killed her?"

"Then you'll figure out who did cause you so damn smart. Listen, Sloan, I know no matter what I do to you right now, you ain't squeakin till you talk to people. We been there."

Un-huh, one real fun time with me handcuffed in the back seat of Booker's county issue in August—windows up, no A/C. And Booker's recollection wasn't exactly spot on: he had indeed squeezed a squeak out of me that episode. As it turned out, the squeak was a big fat lie, so maybe Booker was right.

"But you always step up, always done me alright at the end. I'm gone give you a couple a days to tell me what's goin on, and I'm expectin to be lookin at your *friend* owns this phone pretty shortly." He held up the evidence bag full of phone in case I didn't know which phone he was referring to.

"Why am I helping you, now?"

"Cause somebody's ass goin to jail over this. I'm bein white with you, lettin you decide how good a friend this man is."

"I'll call you if I can find him. Obviously he doesn't have a phone." I pointed at Booker's hand, the one holding the evidence bag.

Booker stopped at his dark-blue unmarked, leaned on the top, spoke over it. "Two days, Sloan, fore we start talkin bout this accessory—you say after the fact—deal. Way I see it, you know who made that call and that puts you halfway there, baby. Let's get busy."

"Fuck you, Booker."

"Nooo, Mr. Sloan. One thing you do not wanna do is fuck me. Not on this deal. You hear me, right?"

I walked, said, "I'll call," over a shoulder. I put pretty much nothing into it that would have encouraged his belief I would actually call.

Didn't have to—he knew I'd call.

Being cute with cops can be fun, but end-report: I'd like to go on hanging shingle in this burg. Add this: as previously stated, the only cop who puts up with my seeming disregard for legal propriety is Lieutenant Detective Mose Booker. Sooner or later I'd call, dad, and he knew I would.

[3]

Forewent breakfast out myself. Just went home to my little apartment, had a couple of soft-boileds on dry toast. Threw a lot of coffee on it.

And there she was, this girl who was nothing but a middle-of-the-night distraction a couple weeks back. Now she was real. She was a throwaway girl in the trunk of a throwaway car. She was dead and I wasn't exactly uninvolved.

I tried letting myself off the hook. Couldn't do it. I'd gone in eyes wide. I'd been in the small blind and I'd foolishly called an all-in, sight unseen. Nothing to do now but look cute and wait out the flop.

Escorted the last of the java out to my garden, slid out of my skids, took myself back—two weeks back, middle of the night. I had to start somewhere and that was the only *where* I had.

★★★

It's true I don't answer my phone much. I've a nice voice-mail option you can select and I consider it my electronic secretary. Way I see it, since the day mankind was blessed with caller-ID, taking calls from unknowns and undesirables became totally, completely and undeniably optional. Leave a message, please.

But sometimes, only sometimes, a number talks to you, says: *Answer me, baby, I'm pertinent.*

Had gone down a little after midnight when the late night guy with the ice-breaker chin started asking nitwits on the streets of LA questions. My opinion of humanity is low enough without watching that shit. REM cycled, woke. Watched the green digits on my bedside companion count off time, flopped, thought about why vandals would take Bob Dylan's handles. No sandman. Two, two-thirty, I'm still lying awake thinking about the government or some feudal shit like that, so my cell, sensing my wretched condition, chirps.

Only a cell-phone chirp, right?

I look at caller-ID. I don't recognize but the bell in the back of my cranium is tolling. At two-thirty, I don't know it's good or ill. I keep looking at the number on caller-ID.

I push a button, say, "Yeah," into the phone.

"Oh, Sloan, I-am-so-fucked."

Hi, hello, how are you? Well, I guess I'm doin fine.

"What's up, Rennie?"

"There's a dead girl in one of my houses."

My mouth wanted to say something stupid like *Whadda you mean dead girl?* but that part of the statement seemed to be traveling handsomely on its own. I said, "What part a town?" It didn't matter—was just something to say.

I repeated the redundant question internally and knew it was wrong, knew I was buying into something toxic.

Rennie named off a nice grid-locked community in our scrub-oak and palmetto suburbs.

"You kill her?" I couldn't imagine it.

"Of course not."

"Calling the cops an option?" I doubted it.

"Un-un."

Ah shit. "This a working house?"

"Big time."

I took long enough Rennie said: "I lose you?"

"No. Thinking." I could hear noise: clicks, thumps. "What're you doing?"

"Jesus, it's hot in here. I'm turning on the A/C. Hang on."

"I'm hanging." Wished I wasn't. "You sure she's dead?"

"Jesus, Sloan, she's got two holes in her forehead. I'd guess *yeah.*"

We paused. I thought. It was two-thirty in the morning, for Christ's fucking sake. I kidded myself some. Thought some more but probably not enough because I said, "She bleed out?"

"Un-huh."

"I know you got a big plastic bag."

"Sure."

"Put her in it. This place have a garage?"

"Un-huh." Rennie was ears up.

"Back in. Put her in the trunk. Go home, park, take a taxi to crack town. Buy a throwaway car off a crack-head. Go back to your house and move her over from your car to the crackmobile. But take her outta the bag—you'll have prints all over it. Park the car somewhere in the sticks. Wipe it down. Walk out at daylight and hitchhike home."

"Sounds like you've put some previous thought to this."

"Gotta think about something on rainy days. Goddam, Rennie, I love ya, baby."

"Same, Sloan. Been a while, huh?"

"Been a minute or two. What? A couple years?"

Rennie laughed some through his nose. "Try three, nearly four. Thanks, Sloan. I owe you. I'll call."

I lay awake some more, thought about the government some more but mostly government incarceration this time. What I'd done was some fucked-up shit. It's called illegal disposal of a body at best—accessory after the fact at worse. Toss in a little bad luck, could put a guy like me upstate at Raiford for the next fifteen years spooning with a fellow felon going by the name of Mandingo, the big sweetie humming obscure Major Lance tunes in my ear.

I felt bad about my scofflaw ways for a short time but got distracted by the emerald numbers on the clock. A few guard changes on the minute side, the sandman popped up, chased me around the bedposts for a very long time. He cornered me port-stern, threw a lazy left jab I laughed off. The jab was only drama—when I looked over, a rocket-powered right hook completed its orbit into my face. My head exploded, became a million emerald fragments. The fragments became numerals and began flowing like a river into a plastic bag the color of nothing. The green fuse sucked my body in after the numbers and I'm pretty sure I died in my dream but woke both alive and contrite the next morning.

Tried not to look at myself in the mirror while I was dragging a brush across my teeth. Couldn't do it.

I pointed the toothbrush at me, said, "You have really fucked up, sweetheart. Big-time fucked up." Spat toothpaste into the sink. "Just wait and see didn't you fuck up big-time."

[4]

Was Rennie someone I'd met in some bar somewhere or a relative of an ex-wife, I'd have tossed him to Booker so fast he'd never remember not being ratted out.

Was Renaldo Alvarez just *someone*, I'd not have clued him on improper disposal of a body in the first fucking place.

Rennie was way back. There weren't many of them. I could count friends and relatives on one fist even back then. As time marched I'd needed less fingers for roll call. Now it was just Ren.

All that weighed, Rennie was more special still. We'd lost our parents together. I was seventeen, Rennie eighteen, summer before our senior year. Next-door neighbors. One bright, cheery August morn the folks, mine and his, sailed out for the old three-hour tour thing—seemingly sailed off the edge of the world for all intents. The authorities didn't have a clue.

A judge allowed Rennie and me to stay put, finish high school. Relatives were to look in on us. All I had was an aunt who looked in on me once, took most of my mom's clothes and jewelry and I've never seen her since.

Rennie's *abuela* moved in with him and watched me like a hawk for hobby, ratting me out to the DCF lady who came by once a month checking on me and Rennie. A few months of that, I made eighteen and any real authority the DCF lady had was all but moot.

We made it out of high-school, went separate directions for higher learning. Rennie applied himself, following his late father into agricultural engineering, whatever that is. I'm sure he learned lots. I pretty well learned nothing but how to roll perfect joints and score quality pussy. A couple of years of that and I took off to Central America, went looking for a guy who'd popped up with Rennie's dad's boat in Limon, Costa Rica.

Rennie went in search of knowledge. I went looking for a Haitian pirate named Pomme de Terre.

Never did find the Potato—and he'd have surely killed my naïve and punkish ass if I had—but I did learn some clever ways to secrete large quantities of marijuana back to the States. Rennie was at Florida International University and was already into small lots distribution. My first super-sized import, Rennie went from selling ounces of swag to moving twenty-pound bales of primo. He embraced the upgrade in circumstance handsomely and we both prospered.

Four, five years, I got sick of the adrenaline and the assholes you got to associate with to work that riff, but, mostly, I think I was just looking for something else and not sure what it was. Got a straight gig at an outfit that looked for lost people and things. Big outfit—rows of filing cabinets with no room for humid Florida air in them. After chasing all over the big blue Caribbean looking for an especially elusive Haitian pirate for a few years, finding motherfuckers in little-bitty South Florida was like gig-fishing in a livewell. Did okay, excelled, got lots of attaboys and pats on the head. Made wads of dough—talking the legal dough. Fucked up and fell in lust with the boss's daughter, compounded the folly by marrying her. Have a beautiful daughter from the union but nothing else is worth a mention one way or another. The ex found out I was an unmotivated, self-centric son-of-a bitch. I found out she was a cunt. Probably wouldn't have worked if we gave it a couple million years.

One afternoon, after Donnie and I had divorced, it occurred to me my father-in-law, whose health would be viewed as not-so-good, would eventually die, leaving this SOB to work for the Cunt. I quit, without proper notice, that moment. Got up, checked my drawers, didn't see shit I couldn't carry on without and walked out with only my nuts. But I did get out with the nuts intact and considered the whole unpleasant script a learning experience. School out.

Not. Went entrepreneurial, tried mixing business and fun by playing truth or dare with a couple of shark-skin suits I met in a bar. It was a nice enough bar, but being Miami, the fucking hoods were stumbling over each other. They were everywhere. The suits and I had shits and giggles over a few white lines, and I ended up doing some fairly clean work for some very dirty people.

As usual, karma caught up with my wayward ass and I did a few minutes Federal time in a different climate. Several changes of lawyers got me homeward bound with a big fat government apology check. Took the legal fucks three years and change, but one of them found a technicality shaped like a key, sprung me. That little fuck's name was Paul C. Mopes, Esquire.

I paid Paulie up and went to ground for nearly a year, trying to put shit in some sort of sane, partitioned order. Never happened so I figured my education was truly complete and moved on to, if not greener pastures, then other pastures.

Rennie followed me out of South-Florida when I made my run. I don't know it was because he thought us brothers or that he was sure I wouldn't be able to embrace the new pious life I'd chosen—now that I was unemployable—and would go back to bringing in bales of square grouper like the good old days.

Didn't happen so Rennie moved on to greener pastures, literally. Blended his education with his affection for the cannabis plant. These days, he bought foreclosed homes in select neighborhoods, cash. Then he'd hire some goober to live there and come and go like regular folk. Next, set up about three quarters of the place in nice high-tech hydroponic-marijuana equipment, box the windows and let the high-pressure-sodium light shine down.

Like growing gold—three bills an ounce and you've got multiple set-ups around town that are rolling out *pounds* of the shit, dad. Reasonable overhead, considering a few months—year at the most—you move the goober and the equipment to another select location, paint the old crib and sell it.

Rennie'd had his own bumps with legality: two short jumps county-time and then he finally managed a ten-to-twelve from a jury of his peers—did nearly six of it straight-up at Raiford. And it looked like he was dead set on getting the State involved in his rehabilitation again.

I knew where his head was. It's easier to quit *doing* dope than it is to quit *selling* dope. Hard times come along? You see dollar signs floating around, waiting for you to grab them. Times get hard enough, you will, too. Then, after a while, I guess you don't know what else you'd do if you didn't do what you'd been doing for the last forever.

Over the past ten years, we'd drifted. Me into hermitic obscurity, Rennie way out past the breakers.

But Rennie was a brother. I had to go look at him, ask him what the fuck was going on. See would he lie to me—see was he still a brother.

[5]

When we the uninspired encounter difficulty, we think point A to point B, go for the path of least resistance which usually involves the obvious. Works for me, anyway.

Slid back in my skids, went inside and grabbed the landline, punched it in the face some. I listened to it purr appreciation as it called a probie I know, big fine Naomi Campbell-looking girl. But there's a trace of Grace Jones in there so she scares hell out of me. Her name is Celeste and she thinks I'm full of mystery and intrigue because occasionally I pretend at being a private eye or something like that.

We flirted and ha-ha-ed some and I asked did she know a Renaldo Alvarez. She said no, wanted to know what would it be worth for her to look him up on her computer.

Told her I'd marry her, father her children. She said she was talking something a little less committal, so I lied, said I'd take her to dinner anytime she chose.

"Right, Sloan. Here's your guy. Sees a parole officer in Seminole County, a Dennis Toussaint."

"What's he reporting for?" I could guess.

"Felony marijuana possession, felony cultivation of marijuana, running a red light and pulling the tag off his mattress. *My.* A friend of yours?"

"Yeah, I think so." We'll see. "Your screen tell you when Renaldo goes in, pisses in a cup for Dennis?"

"Next Monday morning, ten o'clock. This personal or part of your private-eye stuff?"

"I'm not sure, sweetheart." We'll see. "You got a current street on this guy?"

"Un-un. Can't do it, lover, not even if you father my children. You still gonna take me out?"

"I'll call this weekend."

"Sure you will, Sloan."

***

Okay, it was Wednesday. I could wait till Monday, intercept Rennie at his probie's. If I was a patient sapiens I could wait.

Patience isn't a beatitude I suffer from.

There was a way. It was steep and hard. But it always led to the promised land.

Called Raleigh Lightstep. He answered with, "Lightstep, Release Unit," and I said, "What's up? Need a new hat?"

Raleigh says: "Five K."

"Fuck you."

"Seven K."

"The fuck are you on?"

"Ten."

"What're you doing?"

"What am *I* doing? I said *five* and you didn't hang up—I wanna see how high you'll let me go before you do hang up."

I hung up.

Called back.

Raleigh identified himself and I said, "Look, Raleigh, this is my ass. No client, no payola, no fat expense account. Booker's flat-out got me by the balls."

Raleigh went all gooey, said, "That case, fifteen large."

I hung up again. Motherfucker.

Poured fresh coffee on the anger; Raleigh called back.

The number was *private* but I knew it was him, calling from his desk at Thirty-Third Street jail.

I said: "We acting like fourteen-year-old girls some more or what?"

"I don't know what you talking about. I'm getting outta here for lunch in one hour exactly. You wanna know where I'll be?"

"I guess I have to."

***

Knew the Fat Panda would be phat. Considering Raleigh and I'd be dining on my nickel, the man would spare no expense. And it was phat. High, pagoda facade outside, half the national treasure of China inside. Enough to make a tourist golly-gosh and just the sort of place you'd expect Raleigh to choose to abuse my wallet.

You couldn't call Raleigh a friend because he prided himself in having none. Met him on a mutual stake-out before one of his jack-boot compadres kneecapped him by accident at a crack-town takedown. Those days, we—the intimidated citizenry—referred to his squad fondly as the DUKE Boys, Sheriff Kerry Bevin's neo-Nazi drug unit. DUKE was a happy little acronym for something civilized sounding I forget right now. Jack-booters in riot gear is what they were, chosen, I'm sure, on sullenness alone.

So one of the DUKEs shoots brother Raleigh, Raleigh gets a full medical ride, but wait now, he then goes back to work, double-dipping at the county jail on Thirty-Third Street trading in riffraff. He's the one takes the money so the loved-one can be redeemed then extricated from the iron maw of the Man.

Apparently being the guy who decides who'll get county breakfast the next morning and who won't doesn't do shit for a sullen nature. Raleigh's still a large angry black man who suffers little to no foolishness.

He was at a table, wearing the green county bag, eating some sort of finger-food. An exclusive looking bottle of wine sat on the table.

I sat, looked at Raleigh's outstretched leg, the one that didn't like to bend. Said, "This rain fucking with your knee?"

Raleigh swallowed. "Three grand, Sloan. And that's only cause you wanna be your own foolish customer and I think it'll be funny to watch. You can kiss my ass all you want, still gone be three K."

"Remind me why I'm giving you three grand."

"Cause you gonna eventually expect me to break some laws—that's how you roll, remember? I just wanna see you got plenty a skin in the game too."

I had something pretty good about the pleasures of impropriety lined up, but Raleigh put up a finger, said, "You keep it up, we'll start at five grand again."

A short Asian man took my order for a Tsingtao. I *xiexie*-ed him, took a long menu wrapped in hygienic plastic he held in a slender, elegant hand. I *xiexie*-ed again and he drifted.

I asked Raleigh what was good while I winced at the entrée costs.

Raleigh said, "Who knows? I can't read Chinese, so I just order by what price sounds good."

Told Raleigh he was a motherfucker.

He said, yeah, he already knew he was, and my Chinese beer showed up.

Raleigh ordered crispy oysters, Manila clams and more spring-rolls. He'd decide on his two entrées later. And, oh yeah, how about some of those scallops, the ones the size of dessert plates. And make it two orders of crispy oyster—cause I was gonna want one and Raleigh wasn't planning on sharing shit with me. Made the waiter's quick black eyes dart back and forth.

I smiled, ordered large hot-and-sour soup and another Tsingtao.

Raleigh topped off his wine—selected and procured, I was pretty sure, by the same method he'd promised to use on his entrées. He sipped, closed his eyes as though he would know good wine. He opened his eyes, said, "Man, that shit tastes expensive. Tell me a nice story here, Sloan, make me feel good about working cut-rate to bail your nappy white ass."

"You got family, Raleigh?" We'd never gotten around to shit like that.

"Some. Why?"

"You go see 'em?"

"None a your damn business do I see 'em."

Which meant, yeah, sometimes but maybe not enough.

"I got one aunt. Don't wanna see her. This guy I need to find? Was my next door neighbor when I was a kid. Our parents turned up missing at sea together..."

"Jesus, Sloan, save that fucking shit for Oprah. I said I'd help, said three thousand dollars, I know I did. Why you wanna burden me with your personal shit I don't wanna hear about?"

"Not gonna get a discount even with a sad story?"

"Un-un. Look out. Here's food."

Raleigh hid appetizers while I told him about Rennie's call, Booker's call, my call to Celeste.

"So this motherfucker calls, and you tell him how to get rid of a body?"

"Pretty much."

"And now you can't find the motherfucker."

"Pretty much."

"*Pretty much* sounds like what a felon says when he's about to fess up. Who owns the phone?"

I shrugged. "No idea." I was betting it was a burner. If it was in Rennie's name Booker would have called him instead of me about dead girls in car trunks.

"You even put any effort on it?"

"No."

Raleigh paused his grazing. "You so much as look in the phone book for this motherfucker?"

"Un-un."

"All you did is call this probie-girl you know?"

"Yeah."

"Sloan, you oughta be ashamed rushing around passing yourself off as a detective. You seriously ain't traced it yet?"

"Un-un. And the state prefers I refer to myself as a crisis abatement consultant." It had been several years since my exoneration, and Paulie still hadn't pried a private shield or a carry permit outta the state—kept losing my paperwork's what I'd hear.

"Gimme it. Gimme the number."

I pulled out my cell, scrolled to Rennie's digits. Read aloud. Raleigh wrote on a napkin. Said, "Spell your homeboy's name for me."

I spelled.

The waiter showed with soup and took Raleigh's finger-point order.

"I get back, I'll work him through Orange County, see has he been fucking up local. I can *check* with Seminole County. If I get nothing outta them and there ain't no public records on your homeboy or on who owns that phone number, you know what's left, right?"

I un-huhed. Said, "That's why I'm buying you this expensive hat, baby." Found an envelope in the back waistband of my pants, tossed it on the table.

Raleigh said, "What's that?"

"Three large. Mostly Franks, a few Ulleys and a few Jacks for good measure."

If Raleigh appreciated my omniscience, it didn't show. The envelope disappeared in the green uniform without him missing a bite.

Next break his mouth got, he said, "I hope this shit breaks like you want it to, bread."

I said I did too.

[6]

Couple hours, couple of beers back at the hutch, Raleigh calls.

"Your old buddy don't show up on my work computer till you get back six, seven years and my girl at the phone company got laid off."

"Nothing else?"

"Un-un. Other than he paroled out to Seminole County, which you already knew on account of all your clever investigative work."

"You call Seminole County?"

"Yeah. Sheriff's office said should I wanna make it official, they can help me out. Only take a couple a days once I get the proper paperwork to them."

"You call the parole officer?"

"Course I did. He saying the same shit as the county, but I'll tell you right now, Sloan, that motherfucker's dirty."

"You make him nervous?"

"Mmm-hmm. Told him I had a Renaldo Alvarez spelling it a little different; was it his man? I give him some bullshit address in Rio Pinar thinking he'll reciprocate. No, he says it ain't his man, hangs up. Hear what I'm saying? The New York-sounding motherfucker hung up on me."

"So where does that leave us?" I could see this dead weather coming.

"Motherfucker got what we need and he won't cough-up? Guess we gotta go git for our own-damn-selves. You want your boy's vital statistics you bout as well get your dark clothes and Hushpuppies out." Raleigh pissed-off and articulating blackly.

"You're saying we gonna visit his office?"

"Hell yeah. Motherfucker hang up on me? Disrespect me like that? Far as he knew I was somebody calling from Orange County Stockade on county business. Hang up on my ass, motherfucker? Hell yeah we going in his office, get what we want. Motherfucker."

"Pick me up, bitch. I'll be the charming man all in black."

"Ain't nothin but some B-and-E, baby."

"You aren't gonna be inclined to shit on his desk or something weird are you, mad at him like you are?"

"Goddam, Sloan..."

***

I drank some beer, ate some left-over wings and wrestled with myself over taking my pistol to break into a government facility. This situation, sticking a piece down your pants seemed like begging the DA for stacked counts should things go awry—I certainly wasn't planning on shooting anyone.

About dark:30 Raleigh pulled in, honked, and I stuck the gat in my cords, hiked out. Maybe, we got caught, I could shoot *myself.*

Raleigh shoved the Acura up I-4 like it was alive. Seventy-five, eighty—never came off it much. Swung left after drifting down an exit ramp like he knew where he was going. A bit more road, Raleigh swung in a parking lot, said: "There it is." He pointed to a bland office suite, pulled back out. A couple of blocks, we U-turned and went as we'd come.

Raleigh caught a cross street, went left. Another quick left became an alley behind our address decorated with a few renegade palmettos, some utility poles and a few big, flip-top garbage containers.

"We got three minutes, Sloan. From the time we get out the car till we back in is three minutes. Fifteen seconds to the door. It'll take thirty to shake the lock. Fifteen to feel the room, deal with security. That leaves you a minute and a half in the file cabinet, fifteen back to the car and fifteen float time." Raleigh dropped the headlights, scoped the lay then tossed the car behind a Dumpster.

"What'll you be doing all that minute and a half?"

Raleigh came from the backseat with a cartoon pistol. "You ain't got time to worry about it. Come on, motherfucker."

We were on the asphalt, moving. Wondered was Raleigh counting off seconds in his head: *one thousand one, one thousand two...* Wondered who was he planning on shooting with the Buck Rogers gat he had flat against a thigh. Wondered what the fuck I was doing here.

Raleigh tickled the lock. The door felt the love and fell away. He said: "Hang on." Pulled a ski mask over his face. Sauntered in like he was invited.

The funny gun came out. Raleigh, swinging it up, aimed. The pistol made a flat *phlabpt* sound. Raleigh swung left. Another flat pop. Raleigh says: *shit.* Another splat.

Raleigh did that twice more, turned on the lights, said, "You can go get your man's address now."

I went in by him. "You shot the cameras?"

"Un-huh." He shucked the ski mask.

"With a high-tech, see-in-the-dark pellet gun?"

"Yeah."

"The fuck do you get shit like that?"

"You heard about the internet, Sloan? They got all kinda shit you can buy you never even knew you wanted. Go find your file, dad, we hurting on time."

Looked under *A* in the long row of file cabinets. No dice.

Looked at name tags on desks. Found *Dennis Toussaint* on one. Borrowed one of Dennis's Wet Ones for going through his desk. Found Rennie's file in a side drawer. Found his address, his home phone. Found a sticky note inside the front flap that had *new cell* and ten digits written on it.

Wrote it all down on my palm, said, "Let's cook." Tossed the file back where I'd found it and nudged the drawer shut with a foot, tossed the Wet One in a common trash bin.

Out the door. Close it quietly with a shirttail. Walk to the car in a rapid-casual stride. Slide in the car. Slide out of the alley.

Two blocks down, we pass two county cruisers, fired up and wailing, going as we'd come.

I said, "Looks like the fucking reprobates are at it again, huh?"

Raleigh said, "Getting so I'm bout scared to leave the house anymore."

[7]

Slept well thanks to two serious mother's-little-helpers and an unencumbered conscience, then took my time getting presentably vertical the next morning. Brewed coffee, good black double-strength Cuban stuff. Put the cream and sugar in the cup, brought it to a boil in the microwave twice, poured some coffee over it. Read the local rag from cover to cover, excepting ads, sports and the obits. And that advice-column shit of course.

Maybe I should write, see could some aging yuppie broad from the super-burbs help me out. *Dear Blabigale: See, a friend a mine called at like two thirty in the morning, said he had a dead girl in one a his high-brow, high-tech hydroponic marijuana grow houses. So, dumb as it sounds, I told him how to get rid a her body and now I'm up St. Crap's Creek without so much as a scuba flipper. What happened then was, this friend left his phone in the car he ditched the girl's body in, see. And now this fat fucking cop name a Booker knows I got the last call on this phone and thinks it would be funny if I was to go out and solve the case for him. Never mind, Blabs. I see, reading my writing, I should just go blow my fucking brains out. But, hey, thanks anyway.* Sign it: *Dearly Departed.*

Instead of writing, I jumped in dungarees, an anarchy tee-shirt and a pair of soft Toms botas. Dead girls seemed to call for hardware—I slid my Smith Nine in an Uncle Mike's inside-the-pants left-hand so I could stick it down the back of my jeans, still pull it right-handed should the occasion demand. Grabbed an extra fifteen round clip only because of the soaring crime rate in America. Draped a black cowboy shirt over it all. I was clean, sober, barely hungover from the narcotics and didn't care a damn who knew it.

Dragged the beat Vette down Columbia, across the corner of the hood. The light at the old shopping strip nabbed me. I'd seen it all before but I couldn't not look over. Was the kind of place you could get your hair processed and straightened, buy a cell phone and some minutes, a Gandhi store where you could get meat pies of suspect origin and single cigarettes and blunt wraps, a shop that had a sign that said *Shoe Repair* but only sold dime bags of decent mids reefer. The building itself was painted a tone of green that couldn't be justified without involving the term *free paint*—a color so hideous even urban blight wouldn't touch it. Out front, old black guys played tonk and dominoes under a concrete picnic shelter; couple of old couches that made your ass itch just looking at them sat in the weather while discarded tables and experienced lawn-chairs watched. It was a gambling Mecca where upwards of twenty, thirty dollars could trade hands any given day. The place intrigued me because I, being white, could never enjoy it in its purest form—see, once I got out of the car, the whole experience would change, everything adjusting to my terminal whiteness.

Caught a left on Bruton before Columbia degenerates into Raleigh Street and then plunges you post-haste into the heart of the inferno itself, the bona fide hood. Took Bruton as far as the tourist bureau will allow it to go before changing its name to Vineland, trying to civilize things before you get to tourist-ville and on down to where the rich folk live. Down where I'd fully expect a Rennie to squat.

His neighbors would be assorted ball chasers with won-the-lotto-again salaries, straight developers, hoodwink developers, lucky lawyers, the emigrant investors, a bare sprinkling of old money, a thug or two and a hedge-funder or two insulating their own kids from the hellish worlds they perennially create, the fortunate children of chicken-farmers and hundred-acre hard-scrabblers yanked kicking and screaming into the new millennium by the hyper-progress we appreciate here—if growth is progress.

A sign going in warned you'd entered a *No Tolerance Zone.* I didn't doubt it a bit. Tolerance would be rare as hens' teeth in these lakeside/lakeview cuts.

I found the speed limit, poked along. Didn't wish to get intolerated.

And there was Rennie's pad. Nicer than mine by about six thousand square feet. A solid three mil if it was sitting on the lake. It was sitting on the lake.

A stucco wall crashed into a set of industrial-strength wrought iron gates. I pulled up to them, honked.

A heavy-set young guy in a redundant coat for late summer in Florida appeared from the left, coming up the nice paver drive. He looked like I was bothering him, fucking up his mid-morning or something.

Just knew he'd say, *yeah*, like it was work.

He said, "Yeah?" but he didn't fall down from the exertion.

"Tell Rennie Sloan needs to talk."

I got wished good luck and deserted without further ado. No one hurried back to the house. I sat on the nose of my old Shark and appraised Rennie's life.

Big predictable stucco box. Long on Spanish iron-work, short on imagination. The required earth-tone paint had been applied with complimentary earth-tone trim. The original landscaping was losing ground to the relentless ten thousand-plus lumens a square foot we're graced with here. Detached four-car off to the left, where the magilla had come from. Maybe he was the stable boy.

Seemed I was beating up on Rennie and his help and wondered was it jealousy or what. Decided it had to be—how else could you explain it?

Not long, the white kid in the loose jacket comes out the front door. He's smiling, pointing a dingus at the gates, motioning me with the other hand.

The gates concede the opulence so I fall in my car and trudge forward enjoying the sweet taste of acceptance.

I hobbled the Vette and fell out with hopes she didn't bleed any of her vital fluids on Rennie's handsome pink pavers.

The jacket had a lackey smile on his mug when I got to him. He said, "You can come in. I'll take you back." More of the subservient smile. "But I'll have to wand you first."

I smiled back, domesticating myself. "Sure, baby. House rules, I guess."

"Yeah, house rules." He seemed to feel pretty bad about it.

We stepped beyond the nice glass door with the egret etched into it and into the foyer. There was a wand on a nice table that sat under a nice painting. The kid nabbed the wand, crackled it to life.

I put my feet apart, held my arms out.

They always start at your feet. He started there.

I pulled the Smith Nine out of the back of my pants, tapped him on the head with it. He looked up, knowing what it was tapping on his skull. I said, "Let's go see Rennie, tell him how fucking rude it is to treat old friends like this."

He was stupid for a bit so I did a come-along motion with the gat. He stood, looked disappointed in himself, looked at me like I was a sneaky motherfucker. Laid the wand down and hiked out.

I followed his jacket down a long hall, rooms on either side from Architectural Digest, into a vast kitchen full of two more magillas.

It took them a bit but they caught on once they scoped my gat.

I moved it up to Jacket's head, grabbed his collar. "Play nice, girls—I'm a guest."

One of the two, a short Latino kid in a leather vest and doo-rag, fell in line, put a neat little machine pistol to my head, grabbed my collar. We choo-choo-ed like that through the kitchen, out through a mud porch, down two steps to a lanai.

A woman looked up from coffee and newspaper. She could have been surprised or not. She was too goddam cool to tell. An ice cube with gray eyes. I'm a sap for gray eyes.

She spoke and I didn't mind at all I had a full-auto Swedish weed whacker resting on my occipital bulge.

"Santos, this is Renaldo's oldest and dearest friend. And you, Larry, what did you do to provoke Mr. Sloan?" No doubt about who was in charge and who was just hired help.

We didn't wait on Larry or Santos to answer. We turned each other loose.

"Mr. Sloan, won't you join me for coffee? Would you care for a breakfast? A mimosa, perhaps?"

I said *coffee* but was thinking other stuff.

"Santos, please, coffee for Mr. Sloan. Larry, you may return to your duties." Still being the lady of the manor.

The palace guard withdrew, left us on our own.

I'm dying here. I ask: "Ukraine?"

She smiles. "No. Belarus."

Parked it in a metal patio chair, one of those that bounce and make your ass look like a Belgian waffle.

Had to know: "Who are you?"

I could see the what. Hair and complexion of a glacier. Slightly almond shaped eyes, them that pale gray, and like perfect diamonds. Small framed, long limbed. No tits to mention but who needs them you got a face like that.

"Iveta. I am..." She stalled and stopped. Then: "I am not sure what I am."

I watched her: "Rennie's not here?"

"No."

"Does Rennie even live here?"

We thought about that. She said: "He is not here very much. We are married, you know."

No, I didn't know. "But he doesn't stay here much?"

She blushed some, looked in her coffee. Maybe she could find an answer in there. "Renaldo needs badly to see you. He says he must talk to someone about these troubles and he says he can tell you anything. Can I?"

"That would be interesting."

Got scolded with the pale eyes but got a smile with it. "I need citizenship..." stalled again.

"And Rennie needs a legal address, and a legal wife makes perfect."

She blushed again, looked at her coffee some more. "Renaldo says you are a private detective."

I admitted to being close.

"So you wonder about things. Now you are wondering if I sleep with him."

"No. I hadn't wondered." Had.

"Your face is perfect when you lie."

Whatever that means. Okay, so: "Do you sleep with him?"

She looked up, the eyes different. "Ask your old friend Renaldo." Having fun with me, but still telling me something without saying it.

Like a perfect commercial break, the Spanish kid showed with my coffee. He looked at me like I'd gotten him sent to the principal's office. He'd probably spit in my coffee. I smiled, thanked him all the same. He ponied up a smile of his own like he'd probably spit in my coffee. Iveta dismissed him with a *thank you.*

"Could you call Rennie, let me talk to him?" There was a well-evolved communication dingus on the table and I pointed at it.

She shook the ashen hair, maybe just shy of shoulder length, points aiming at a delicate chin. "Renaldo said if you came here to tell you he had—what is it?—done the mattress?"

"Gone to the mattresses."

"Yes. He said he would call you."

I nodded slowly, watched the neglected cup of joe in front of me. "Tell him I've got his new cell number and I *will* be calling his ass." Looked up at her. "And I *will* find his ass."

She smiled ever so slightly, said, "I would love to know what are your troubles with Renaldo."

I said, "Who says I got troubles with Renaldo?"

Sounded dumb to me, and she knew it was dumb.

She said, "Does everyone call you Duncan?"

"No, everyone calls me Sloan."

"You are not bad, Sloan. You would be easy to get used to. You should probably go."

I don't know what to say—I'm straight-up thinking from the dick right now.

Was nothing I *could* say wouldn't sound like a weak barroom pick-up line. I said, "Bye," made my drift. Top of the steps, before I stepped through the mud-porch doorway, I turned.

She was smiling. And it wasn't a Sunday school smile. What it was was a smile could make a sketchy motherfucker want to jump his best friend's wife. Felt it all the way down to the remote end of my zipper.

I shook my head, smiled back. No, you couldn't have taken my smile to Sunday school either. Time to go, Sloan—your tongue's hanging out.

I said, *bye*, again, got the hell outta there.

The three young gunsels were roosting in the big professional kitchen again.

The two I'd been intimate with, the large white kid in the big jacket and the Latino, glared at me. The other, a tall yellow-toned black kid, thought it was all pretty fucking funny.

I tossed a, *hasta la vista,* at them.

Spanish-blood says, "No, no need to come back, bro." Some semi-authentic glare, B-movie shit he'd seen on the high-numbered cable channels. "You need to listen to me, *tio*."

I stopped, shook my head. Looked at the punk, Aunt Jemima's dishtowel around his chunky head. "You don't learn to lighten up, you ain't gonna make it in this game, baby. I ain't your uncle and I damn sure ain't your bro. You don't know *who* the fuck I am, but you choose to disrespect me all the same." I smiled. "Need to learn how to hold on to those nuts, don't let 'em drag you around. Makes you look silly to the rest of us."

The black kid thought it was way funny.

I said, "Ain't that right, Sambo?"

Just a second, just a nano-flash, he wanted to kill me. He smiled good teeth at me, said, "You're ice cold, *tio*."

I looked back at Spanish. "See? That's how you do it. Keep smiling at the motherfucker—he won't ever see it coming. Bye, babies. Don't grow up to be cowboys or nothin."

There was so much juice in the room, all of it directed at me, it made the hairs on the back of my neck pirouette as I walked out.

***

Halfway crib-wise, Raleigh cells me.

I go: "Yeah?"

He says: "You find your boy?"

"Un-un."

"Then, baby, I believe I earned my whole piece today."

Jesus—Raleigh damn near excited? Maybe I should pull over, get out and look up, see if the sky's falling. "Talk to me, dad. Tell me good things."

"Our guy, Dennis Toussaint?"

"Un-huh. The one you hate."

"Fuck you. You wanna hear this shit or we gone tell jokes?"

"Speak."

"Then behave. This motherfucker calls—turns out, he's from New Jersey instead of New York—motherfucker says: *You want it bad enough you break in my office, me and you need to talk.* I say: *We talking now.* Told me your friend's floating in money but if I'm looking to move in, let's me and him talk about it—make sure ain't nobody fucking the golden goose too hard, see. Told you, Sloan. This motherfucker's dirty as backyard worms."

"Nice. You ask him why he thinks it's you that broke in?"

"Un-huh. He says I called, then somebody breaks in all clean and professional, don't take nothing, just rummaged through his desk, messed with Alvarez's file."

"Say how."

"Fuck, Sloan, I don't know how he knew. Maybe he's got some Double-Oh-Seven way a closing his fucking desk drawer. I didn't see pursuing it was gonna get me anywhere. I just asked him what exactly he had in mind. He said we should get a drink after he gets off today."

"So, you tell him to fuck off? Tell him you're not that sorta public servant?"

"Right. Gotta meeting this evening with the gentleman."

"Remind me what we're getting outta this now?"

"We gone get this boy Dennis to put us in front of your friend."

"Why's he gonna do that?"

"Cause you gone pay him well."

"*Reasonably* well. What if *he* ain't that sorta boy? You gotta plan for that?" I just knew he did.

"Yeah, I gotta plan for that. You got any heavy zip-ties?"

[8]

Booker caught me back at the shack. I dodged the call but pulled it up on voicemail immediately. Nothing new: I was running out of time.

Fuck it. Bumped him back. Honestly? I wanted to see if he'd been able to trace the phone to Rennie yet. I doubted such.

He came on, said, "Mr. Sloan. Tell me sump'n I didn't know fore you called."

"Need a bit more time, Booker."

"Un-huh. That's what I was afraid of. Sure was."

"You said a couple a days."

"Un-huh. They was all day yested'y and then here's today. Where we at, Sloan?"

"I should have this guy's location by this evening, hook or crook. Can we talk tomorrow?"

"What if I say no?"

"Same—we'd still be talking tomorrow."

"What I thought. You ain't gone let this fucker fly to avoid prosecution are you?"

"Booker, he was your friend and he needed to fly, what would you do?"

"My friends ain't the same as your friends."

"They are to me and, just like you, I'll respond according to my own fucked-up definition of justice should that situation arise."

"You always do, don't you? Listen, I want you at the big buildin, eight in the mornin, and I don't want no shit about it either. I got somebody you need to meet. Bring your man should he show up."

"Look, Booker, straight dope: I haven't seen the guy, haven't talked to him. I found his legal residence, met his wife, got a meeting with his parole officer."

"Parole? Where he paroled out to?"

"Seminole County. Hang tight. I'll find him."

"That's what you keep sayin, but I keep lookin up and ain't you nor him neither one standin in front a me. I need a name, Sloan, need a name."

"Who was the phone registered to?"

A pause, then: "Was a burner, registered to a Missus Everly at a lot ain't got nothin on it but a light pole and some sandspurs. Talk to me, Sloan."

"*Manãna*, Booker."

"Tomorrow, Sloan. And don't you fuck me." A little chuckle. "Your *own fucked-up definition of justice.* You a fuckin mess, Sloan. Don't fuck me."

He was gone and I was glad.

Grabbed a beer. Full of no optimism, I dialed the cell number for Rennie I'd glommed from his parole jacket.

Ring.

Ain't gonna happen.

Ring.

Gonna get: No one here—leave a message.

Ring.

Come on, Rennie.

Ring.

Oh well.

Mechanical Rennie saying how I could leave a message.

I go: "Rennie, motherfucker, you need to call me like now. I got cops all over me and I ain't too illegal these days. I won't cover you it gets too hot. Call, bitch."

Killed it.

Sat around, tried not to think too much about why a guy who had three thugs hanging around his kitchen with artsy automatic weapons, a guy had enough of a crew to *do the mattress*, would call me, middle of the night, over something as trivial as a dead girl. Why would a guy who had lived on the dark side so long be so careless as to leave a cell phone in a car full of dead girl? I'm a skeptic, so most coincidences seem outlandish to me, but I was trying like a motherfucker to give Ren the benefit of all the doubt. It was getting harder to do all the time. Wouldn't let myself think beyond grand coincidences and I knew I was probably fucking up.

Raleigh rang back. Some *Hey*, he says: "Six o'clock. Bombay Bicycle Club."

"When did you start going in fern-bars?"

"Who's going in? Ain't nothing inside but phony white people and eyewitnesses."

"You sure on this, Raleigh?" I'm thinking this isn't much less crazy than shitting on the guy's desk.

"See you at five-fifteen. I'm in the Lincoln."

"What Lincoln?"

"The big one. I'm done using my car to do your dirty so I picked up something disposable. Hey, bring them padded gloves I loaned you. We on a tight schedule—don't be a girl," and Raleigh was gone.

Padded gloves? Big zip-ties? Ah, man. Ain't nothin but a little felonious assault and some light kidnapping, looked like.

***

Raleigh blows in, toots. I walk out, take a look.

An eighties Lincoln. Ugly-ass, blue, big as a whale. Newer fabric top—not a rag-top but one of those fake ones. Cherry inside like it had been some tuner's girlfriend at one time. It was interesting. I got in and said so.

"Twelve hundred. Got you a deal." Raleigh put the barge on the street, driving a little faster than my neighbors admire.

It sinks in. I pause. Then: "This is my car?"

"Un-huh. And you owe me twelve. She do run sweet, don't she?"

I put my feet on the dash like I owned the sled. "Good luck on the twelve."

Raleigh stopped, did a neat back-in three-point in a driveway.

"Where you going?" I slid my feet off the dash.

"Drop your cheap ass back at your crib, see how much a your money I can get back on the car."

"Jesus. I need to sign a change-order or something?"

"You gone pay me the twelve?"

"Yes." Fuck.

Raleigh did another three-point, got back on our *tight schedule*. Made me wonder did he float in a minute, forty-five seconds to get the twelve hundred outta me.

Of course he did. I put my feet back on the dash of *my* Lincoln Town Car.

★★★

Raleigh placated the presidential beast under a scrawny mall shade tree that wasn't shading anything including itself. Our perch afforded us view of most of the parking lot. What we couldn't see bugged fuck outta Raleigh and he kept complaining about it.

"How are you gonna know this guy?"

"He's in a black Lexus."

"Funny how government employees all over keep showing up in high-end Japanese automobiles."

"Don't change your taxes none, no matter what I do, nor what this motherfucker does." Got a Raleigh-beat, then, "I bought that Acura—cash—off what I made fucking with you last couple, three years." He'd have laughed if he was a laugher.

I didn't even look over to see if he was grinning. The fascist fuck doesn't grin much, but something like that could get him happy.

A black Lex showed, finished making Raleigh's day perfect.

"Sit tight." Raleigh bailed out, walked across the asphalt to intercept the car as it committed to a space.

The rearview on my side gave a look. Some chat between Raleigh and a short stocky guy in a loud silk shirt and loose dark slacks. The mirror couldn't hide the guy's opinion of himself, him thinking he had style but really having little to none. Wore his hair back and shiny. Wore cheap, wrap shades off the rack at like Walgreens or somewhere. Penny loafers; no socks. Had a wristwatch only slightly bigger than a manhole cover.

He put out a hand Raleigh ignored. Instead, Raleigh used his hand to point in my direction. The two of them came my way.

When they were close I could hear Raleigh telling the guy something about the Lincoln's cavernous trunk.

I'm thinking, *oh shit.*

Raleigh jingled a key, used it on the trunk.

A small amount of scuffling and the trunk lid was closed. No one in the mirror now but Raleigh, then I lost him until he came around, got in.

Raleigh cranked the car and backed out conscientiously while me and a couple of my elevated eyebrows watched him.

"He didn't mind riding in the trunk?"

"I tased him. He'll be coming around." A thoughtful nod. "He comes around he may mind."

"You tased him?"

"Hey, you the one didn't have no zip-ties."

Raleigh crossed the Interstate, went left, going as we'd come.

"And you were the one said we were gonna bribe him."

"Didn't fall that way."

"You even ask him?"

"He didn't seem like the type. Just put him in the trunk. We get him out, you wanna give him some money, go ahead on."

"Why? You tased the motherfucker and put him in the trunk now."

Four, five miles, I noted how quiet our passenger was. Asked Raleigh was this how the tasing people and chunking them in the trunk usually went.

Raleigh said, "Pretty much. Right now, he thinks he's gone die. Thinks we taking him to the landfill or somewhere. He's thinking what he's gone do when we get there. We get off the big road, he'll try something."

"You gotta plan on that?"

"Uh-huh."

My neighborhood exit came up. Raleigh used a right-hand blinker. Half-way or so down the off-ramp, he whipped over to the breakdown lane, then onto the grass. Quick, out of the car, around to the trunk. The trunk lid pops up.

I couldn't understand Raleigh's mumble, but the guy in the trunk said, "Don't tase me, brother-man."

Ough. Don't call large angry black men *brother-man*, brother-man. The guy screamed, the trunk lid went closed.

Raleigh slid in, drove on with what I thought was an absolutely tranquil demeanor. I watched the side of his face, envied the serenity the little psychopathic episode had lent him.

Bottom of the ramp, he goes right. I lived to the right, a fact I felt entitled me to say: "You're not taking that motherfucker to *my* house."

Raleigh looked over, a funny grimace that may or may not have been a smile.

"For three measly grand, I've broken into a government facility, destroyed state property, assaulted and kidnapped a state employee. Oh, and improper use of my position to illegally obtain classified information."

"I know, Raleigh, and I feel terrible about it. Wasn't that what the three hundred dollars worth of unreported Szechwan from the Fat Panda was: informational services? You want, I'll give you a receipt saying so, but you're still not taking the motherfucker to my house."

"You gone cry, what the baby gone do, Sloan? We going to my ex-wife's home."

"Ex-wife? I didn't know you were ever married."

"Lotta shit about me you don't know cause it ain't none a your fucking business."

"She home?"

"Un-uh. She's in Europe or somewhere doing her corporate shit."

"She doesn't hate you?" My experience said ex-wives hated ex-husbands.

"Nah, we cool. She travels, I check on her crib, drink her wine, lay on the leather sofa—shit I couldn't do when we were married."

"Lucky you."

Raleigh pulled in a drive across from a small, suspiciously indigenous-looking lake, the lake maybe five acres and blessed more with cypress and cattail than hydrilla.

The drive was salted concrete lined with old brick, rows of brick at dissecting intervals. Rambling ranch meets modern Florida: stuccoed-over and barrel-tiled. Enough landscaping to drain the lake twice a week just keeping the sun from turning it all to dust. Raleigh's ex had herself a damn nice place on a nice lake in a convenient downtown enclave.

I rented two, three blocks west. Bet Raleigh's ex didn't rent. Corporate-and-world traveler she was, she probably didn't even have a silly old mortgage.

Raleigh flipped the sun visor, pressed a garage-door gadget.

The door rose. Light shone.

Dennis Toussaint began kicking and yelling. Some noise about, *Help, I'm being killed,* or something like that.

"You planning on killing him?"

Raleigh put up a *hadn't-thought-about-it* face, shrugged barely. "I guess that'd be up to him."

The Lincoln rolled in the big finished garage. A few garden items hung on a neat pegboard; other stuff that couldn't hang—pots and bags of potting soil and fertilizer—sat on a high wooden work table. Couple of cardboard boxes, both two-foot cubes, stacked by the table. Air handling unit on a white plenum. A bike hanging on a hook like a gaffed fish. Egress door to the outside with a small window in it. An older chest freezer—rounded corners like it came from Grandma's when she died—that had been repainted poorly. A traffic door led into the house, I could presume.

Raleigh says, "Hang tight."

We sat as the door came down. When it bumped, Raleigh popped his door, turned to exit.

"You gotta plan, right?"

Raleigh un-huhed, got out.

I de-carred. Over the vast top of the sled, Raleigh says: "You gone love this. I been waiting for the opportunity to show you, knowing how you'd be someone could appreciate it."

Man, I couldn't hardly wait. Said so.

Raleigh went over to the freezer, removed a long padlock from the chromium handle, stuck the lock in a back pocket. Opened the freezer.

I'm thinking, *oh shit*, slash, *not fucking bad, baby,* all at the same time.

Raleigh goes over, pops the trunk. The guy comes up cursing, pointing a finger in Raleigh's face. Raleigh grabs the guy—he's a little Joe Pesci-looking fucker—by his collar and his belt, picks him up and carries him over to the freezer. Toussaint's cursing and threatening the whole sad trip.

Knowing Raleigh's gonna put the little motherfucker in the freezer. Yep, tossed him down in there like a bag of sugar peas. Slammed the lid, slid the lock from his back pocket through the handle. Turned, said: "How you like it so far?"

"What can I say? You're simply amazing. You're both a gentleman *and* a psycho, dad. I've tried it and it's no easy task."

Raleigh thanked me, said, "I'm gone have me a glass of some fine Chateau Yqem. You want me to see can I find you a beer?"

"Brown if available. Wet if not."

Raleigh used the traffic door and I could hear him playing notes on a security pad.

I looked at the freezer, said, "Oh, Dennis, Dennis, Dennis, you ought not have hung up on Raleigh. See how shit can happen you don't even think about when you go fucking with under-medicated individuals?"

There was some thumping about from the freezer but not what you'd expect, not as much as I'd be thumping was it me in there. Then it got quiet.

I looked at my watch, wondered if I should be keeping time or something.

Raleigh showed, a brandy snifter full of pale wine and a Harp. The beer got poked at me. "That do? It's brown ain't it?"

The bottle was brown. "Close enough."

Raleigh took his snifter over to the freezer.

Time to redeem Dennis Toussaint?

Nope. Raleigh turned, sat the snifter on the freezer and slid himself onto it. "Sit down, Sloan."

I gave him a face that required him to say: "I don't know. I'm playing it by ear. Way his body's distributed, I bet he could go three, four hours fore he actually goes to sleep. But I believe frostbite'll set in his extremities sooner than that at them low temps and he'll go to complaining about the pain."

"Cool. You keep time—he didn't hang up the phone on me like he did you. Man's nothing but a means to an end to me." I shrugged at that, hopped on the hood of the Lincoln. Sipped a Harp that had been hiding in the fridge a tad too long, but wasn't overly skunky for a late-afternoon freezer party.

Raleigh didn't have much to say. Guess he was too busy keeping up with how long the guy'd been in the chiller, though I didn't catch him doing it.

Another beer and a bit, I asked, "What's up with that?" pointing at the freezer.

"Quiet, ain't he?"

"How long you thinking?"

"Hell, I don't know. You ain't never locked anybody in a freezer before either, have you?"

I thought about it, asked, "Does a walk-in count?"

[9]

A second snifter of wine, a third not-too-skunky Harp, and it looked like show time.

Raleigh belched, slid off the freezer, knocked a couple of stout knocks. No response so he pulled the padlock out of the handle, opened the freezer.

Frost swirled up, Dennis Toussaint appeared in a mist fit for gorillas. The guy had long bags, like bread bags, on his hands, up his arms. He'd wrapped some kind of freezer paper around himself. There were meat stains on the paper.

The bitch looked cold but he came up yakking. I could only assume the man insane or terribly out of his comfort zone, out of his region of reason, if you will.

He was ratcheting out some shit about how he was gonna get Raleigh ten, fifteen years for this shit. How Raleigh—calling Raleigh *Brother Lightstep*—had fucked up sooo bad.

Raleigh had fucked up sooo bad he slapped—open-handed bitch slapped—the big-mouthed little fuck, closed him up in the freezer again. Slid the padlock in the handle.

Said: "You want another beer, dog? I think there's one more."

"Sure, baby. This takes longer than holding a guy's head in the sink."

"Yeah, but it's so much more civilized."

I shrugged. "Times change. I met you, you had that slick-sidewalls, eraser-head fro and still dated white women."

Raleigh said I remembered too good, disappeared into the house again.

Dennis was yelling something; I couldn't decipher and didn't care much. This deal seemed to be between Raleigh and Dennis Toussaint with me serving as casual observer only. I wished I were enjoying it less.

Civilized beasts we'd become, Raleigh and I ignored Toussaint's dilemma, savored our libation, small talked about nothing more important than fish bait as men will do.

Raleigh's sensibilities cued him to check on Toussaint, see was he chilled enough to act civilized, civilized like Brother Lightstep and me.

The freezer door came up, Toussaint didn't.

I was hoping Raleigh hadn't fucked up, killed the little guy or something, him being government and all. If the fucker was dead, I also didn't think I'd get the much sought after meet-up with Rennie.

Raleigh leaned over the freezer, said, "Dennis, my man, you ready to behave yourself, talk to us?"

A quiet, *yeah*, came from the icy box.

"Well, come on, then," like a patient parent.

Raleigh reached in, pulled Toussaint up and out, stood him beside the freezer. The little guy was stiff and wobbly all at once. His eyes looked at nothing. He slumped to the floor, his back against the freezer.

"Jesus. I thought I'd died." He slid the bags off his arms, lolled his head around.

"I can arrange it, Dennis, you go to acting out some more." Raleigh closed the freezer.

Toussaint pulled the freezer paper away, let it fall on the garage floor. "No. I'm good, I'm good." He flexed his fingers slowly, reached up, touched his rosy cheeks. "I can't feel my face."

"It's still there. You need a shot a whiskey?" Raleigh being the perfect host.

"Oh, man, do I."

Raleigh came back with a bottle of Pinch, started Toussaint off with a coffee cup full. The man shook half of it on himself, but got the rest down.

Cup out for more, Raleigh obliged.

Toussaint started gagging, leaning over like he was gonna chuck.

Raleigh said, "Don't you puke, motherfucker. You puke you gone clean it up."

Toussaint got it together, slapped his chest, breathed deep. "The fuck you put me in the fuckin freezer for?" It wasn't snappy like before. He was beat, he was downtrodden. He'd been wrongfully abused.

"You got information we need and you acting like a dick. We can pretty much do what we want with you, see? I'm working for Orange County on a grant, Federal grant." A point to me. "Right there is Agent Duncan, Homeland Security, Dennis. Get it? He says I wanna put your ass upside down on an ironing board, pour water up your nose, it's fine. He's observing, see, make sure I don't go too far. Ain't that right, Agent Duncan?"

Man, what a silver-tongued devil Raleigh was all of a sudden. I smiled like a DHS agent, said, "Absolutely, Lightstep. Use any means you need—I need a pronto locate on this Alvarez individual."

Dennis Toussaint wasn't a dunce. He studied me like I was a picture of me, like I wasn't animate. I didn't mind. Let him put it through the sieve.

A big sip of whiskey, another mimed request for more.

Rewarded with scotch whiskey.

Then: "This fuckin guy ain't no terrorist. He's a fuckin marijuana farmer. Big-time farmer."

I crossed my legs officiously. "We're aware of Mr. Alvarez's chain of grow houses, Mr. Toussaint. Not that it's any of your concern, but my division's specialty is the drug connection to overseas money. We've got a solid connection to your client—he's been exchanging wads of Syrian pounds, unaccounted-for Syrian pounds."

Toussaint was feeling the Pinch, said, "You gotta badge, ID card or somethin, Mr. Duncan? No offense, but you really don't look like..."

I jumped him: "Toussaint, you're in no position to be making requests. You're under interrogation at the moment. I really wish you'd seen your way to cooperate. Proceed, Lightstep."

"Whoa. Whoa, fellas. We don't need to proceed with shit here. What? You need to catch up to this Alvarez guy? Shit, you got him. Fuck. That's all you want and you gotta stick me in the fuckin freezer?" Getting some jump back in his game.

"Shut up and drink your scotch, Dennis." Raleigh looked at me. The fucker so wanted to smile, I know he did.

Toussaint wanted to know where we were.

Raleigh reminded Dennis how he'd told him to shut up and drink his fucking scotch.

[10]

Scotch, greed or a combo of both had Dennis Toussaint in peril again.

When he mentioned bucks, it seemed like more fun to watch Raleigh.

Raleigh reached down, got a hank of the little man's hair to yank Dennis upright. Raleigh's hand came away with the hair.

Raleigh and I watched his handful of scalp, looked at each other, looked at Dennis.

Dennis was feeling his bald head.

"Christ, man, you just snatched off a thousand dollars worth of hair weaving."

"Dennis, I'll snatch the goddam skin off your head you don't quit disrespecting us."

"How's asking for a little compensation disrespect?"

Easy, Dennis. That whiskey-fed greed's gonna bring you grief. See if it won't.

Dennis's collar didn't pull off like his hair when Raleigh pulled him up by it.

I could have watched this perversion all day but time was short. Raleigh opened the freezer and tossed Dennis in again and I said: "You know, Lightstep, I may be able to get Mr. Toussaint some compensation if he cooperates from here on out."

"Dennis, you hear the man?" Raleigh was still in control of Dennis's left foot.

Dennis mumbled from down in the freezer and I didn't catch it.

"He says you quit acting the fool and showing out, he may can get you some money."

Raleigh looked at me, bother and trouble contorting his face. He pushed Dennis's foot in, closed the freezer's lid.

"What'd he say?"

"The motherfucker wanted to know how much you was talking, like he might choose the freezer if it wasn't enough. Man, ya'll some fucked up people."

"Who's *ya'll*?"

"White people."

"What? You waiting on me to argue that point? Let the motherfucker out." I could hear Dennis tapping politely inside the freezer.

Raleigh opened the lid.

Dennis appeared timidly.

I said: "Four grand."

Dennis said: "Five, and we gotta deal."

I said: "Close the lid, Raleigh."

Dennis conceded the grand.

Didn't matter: it was all imaginary government money anyway. I could put in an imaginary request and have Dennis's imaginary four grand in a week or so.

Dennis would have liked more immediate gratification but understood how the system worked. His understanding made Raleigh happy enough he lifted Dennis out of the freezer and stood him on the floor.

"What is it, exactly, you're needin me to do, now?"

My face smiled, said, "Call Alvarez. Set up a meet. Let him choose the spot—we don't want him suspicious. That's all I need, Mr. Toussaint."

Dennis patted himself down, said, "I've lost my phone."

Raleigh produced it from a pocket. When Dennis's hand neared, Raleigh snatched the phone back.

"Dennis, I believe this'll go better you was standing in the freezer while you made this call. You know, remind you what could happen you get cute."

"Cute? Man, for four grand I'd stand on my head and bark like a fuckin seal."

Raleigh passed him the phone, said, "Dennis, behave yourself."

***

It pissed Toussaint that Raleigh made him get back in the trunk. I personally never thought for a moment Dennis would leave Raleigh's ex-wife's home in a sitting position. Dennis complied, under protest, but only after being threatened with further tasing.

And I knew Raleigh wasn't done fucking with the guy yet. Hey, he'd hung up on Raleigh once upon a time.

A little of this way, a little of that way, and Raleigh stopped in a tired old industrial area, popped the trunk.

The car bobbled a bit.

Raleigh put his window down, said, "Close the trunk, Dennis," and did the window up.

The trunk clicked shut and Raleigh drove off, leaving Dennis in the pale glow of the twilight.

"You think he knows where he is?" I wasn't sure I cared.

Raleigh shrugged out an equal lack of concern. "He'll find out soon enough."

Dennis was surrounded on four sides by raw concentrated peril. No matter which way he walked, he'd surely be talking to bangers and lead-slingers before he got a ride out.

"You're a vengeful fucker, know it?"

"Does seem like it, don't it?"

Raleigh didn't put much in it to make me think he'd change his evil ways.

[11]

Rennie had dodged Dennis's call at Raleigh's ex's shack, just like he'd done mine. But, he'd been concerned enough to hit Dennis back in a minute or two. I'd had an almost-overwhelming urge to snatch the phone from Dennis, call Rennie a motherfucker and ask him what the fuck he was doing.

Passed on the emotions: I'd ridden this train to here, why change up? Rennie would have just hang up and continued to dodge me. And I was glad I did—Dennis had pulled it off nicely. He had told Ren the Feds were wrapping him up and he needed traveling dough. He was going on a long vacation, burn up some accrued leave till shit chilled.

Rennie was reluctant but Dennis had been both clever and motivated if not particularly smart. He'd lied about having some inside shit to relay to Ren but was afraid to talk over the phone.

Ren conceded, picked a rest area that was well lit and well Wackenhutted out on the Four, toward Tampa. Said ten o'clock which had only been an hour and a half away.

It had sounded like a plan, and we acted accordingly after tossing Dennis. Even showed up early so as to get a good seat. Wasted effort—coulda pretty much had any seat we wanted.

Three big rigs in a front lot by the freeway, a camper rig keeping them honest. The facility separated the truck lot from the regular parking area. Only two cars there and they looked lonesome on all that asphalt.

A guy in a rent-a-cop outfit looked even more lonesome out there on all that asphalt.

Raleigh caught the picnic lane to the backside of the lay, hobbled my Lincoln a couple of spaces from the end. We watched the rent-cop finish his outside rounds and move to the facility building.

It was quiet for a bit but for Gill Scott-Heron laying some quiet stylings on us from Raleigh's sound selections. Seemed there was a great big time bomb tick, tick, ticking up in South Care-o-lina.

A boxy black SUV showed, pulled around to the side parking area, took the last slot on the right. Its lights went down and no one got out.

Quiet again now but for The Last Poets insisting negroes wake up.

Another vehicle, a caddy the color of smoke, pulled in and took the last slot on the left, directly across from the SUV. Raleigh silenced the Poets. Said: "This may get interesting."

I wished it hadn't parked where it did. Doing so created a worrisome bottleneck to anyone hoping to leave the car park area.

Raleigh was keying up on the same thing. He said, "You got that piece a shit Smith and Wesson small caliber on you, don't you?"

I carry a Smith 5905, a near-antique fifteen-round 9 mm. If I can't kill you with the fifteen rounds, it makes a good club. Raleigh carries high-dollar, high-tech shit, nothing less. To him, 9 mm had become small arms.

I told him, yeah, I had it.

He asked how many clips I'd brought.

I shrugged.

Raleigh shook his head. I'm sure I was in store for a good dressing down about my slack ways which would degrade into a complaint for working so cheap, but a car, a glittery low-rider, stopped on the interstate break-down lane. Someone exited, said some good-byes. The car sped away; the passenger turned and walked toward rest area lights.

Raleigh raised nocs, said, "Shit."

"What?"

Raleigh hands me the nocs, I take a peek.

Dennis Toussaint had found a ride and a ball cap. Then he was crossing the truck lot, then he disappeared behind the building.

I said, "The fucker's gotta be deranged." Got out, stretched, walked up to where I could see Dennis for a bit longer. The building shielded him again but it seemed he went inside the facility.

Took the opportunity to piss behind the last picnic table. Was shaking it when a tall mud-bogger careened in, horn honking.

The truck never tried to turn when the asphalt all flowed left. It jumped the curb, veered dangerously, came back around in control. The driver gunned the motor, eating up the landscaping in big chunks. Couple of doughnuts got cut in the lawn before the security guy came running out. He yelled, tossed a cup of something and pumped it for the truck, hand on his flapping gat. He yelled again. The truck broke from cutting circles, stopped, then took off. The rent-cop yelled. The truck stopped again. The rent-cop trotted by the SUV and into the dark.

As the rent-cop passed the SUV, a door popped, a guy stepped out and quietly shot the rent-cop twice in the back with a muffled piece. The truck used the exit and was no more.

I started running for the Lincoln. I looked back and watched the guy walk over and quietly put one in the security guard's skull cap.

At the car, I told Raleigh, "Take the bulb outta the light."

Raleigh held the bulb up.

I popped the door in the darkness, got in. Raleigh and I watched three guys in leather coats roll the guard up in a sheet of plastic. Then, they humped him to the fence and tossed him in the weeds on the other side. They sauntered back to the SUV, loaded up.

Raleigh went philosophical, said, "Mmm-mmm-mmm. Motherfucker come to work and get dead for—what?—ten dollars an hour?"

"What're you thinking?"

Raleigh gave it a few beats, said: "I'd say they waiting on your friend Renaldo."

"Or Dennis sold us, and they're Rennie's guys waiting on me and you."

"We starting to doubt your friend's sincerity?"

I grunt some affirmative, so Ren shows in an innocuous, inconspicuous, two-hundred-large worth of Ferrari.

I slapped at Raleigh. He said, "Un-huh. I see him. Boy knows how to stay low-key, don't he?"

"Maybe that's a disguise."

"It is, it's a good one. Who'd be looking for a drug dealer in an Italian race car?"

I watched Dennis appear under the overhang, wave at Ren. "Shit."

Rennie followed the parking lot as it went left, stopped. Dennis came his way.

I said, "Fire it up, Raleigh," and dug a handgun outta my pants.

Raleigh said, "Hold on. Either Dennis's about to get dead or me and you going through that fence over there and then through that orange grove when they come after us."

Dennis leaned on Rennie's high-dollar dago steel like he was pretty cool.

The dark Caddy cranked, backed up to within a couple of feet of the SUV, went quiet. Then two doors opened on the SUV. A door opened on the Caddy stalled in the drive. Three overdressed guys got out like harmony itself. They'd grown some efficient looking hardware. The crew spread out a little, brought their front sights up.

I started yelling at Rennie to get the fuck outta there.

No way he heard me, but he did as though he had: went brake lights first in a cloud of smoke, left Dennis Toussaint like Dennis was toting the typhoid germ.

The shit hit. Sparks on concrete, car and pavement. Dennis jigged a high-step, went to his knees. More lead. Dennis gets excused from the scene, kisses asphalt.

Ren hit the curb, jammed gears with a painful grinding. Slowed, readdressed the clutch, left the whole affair like Halley's Comet, going the way he had come, traveling against the one-way signs.

The gunsels slung some random cap at Rennie, wised up and ran toward the highway.

Ren's Ferrari showed on the highway, accelerating like gravity and friction had taken a holiday. Automatic weapons chattered and flashed vainly in the dark. The Guinea go-cart was, then it wasn't.

A rubbernecker had gotten out of one of the cars, rousted by the noise I figured. A trucker was on the tarmac watching the scene unfurl like it was satellite TV.

The gun goons turned, walked back to the guzzlers. Some tête-à-tête, one of the goons makes a move, lifts like he's gonna pop the trucker, then sights down on the car-lane guy. Both innocent unfortunates run like motherfuckers for their respective vehicles. Our hardware boys load up, ease off into the mum and starry night.

Raleigh says: "You want 'em?"

"Not that bad, not with the heat they're toting."

Raleigh said: "You want 'em, I got shit in the trunk can hang with 'em."

"I bet you do. Nah, let's just tag along, see where they light."

"You know what's gonna break should they figure we're back here."

"Un-huh. Somebody's probably gonna get shot. We don't have to get close enough to steal their shoes, dog."

Raleigh asked did I want to drive. I told him no, I was fine supervising over here.

He fired up the Lincoln, tossed the shifter to *drive.*

Nice—a county cruiser rolls in, parks rudely, ejects a doughnut-fed public servant. He digs his drawers outta his ass crack, hikes his Sam Browne set-up, makes for the facility.

The witness from the car gets out, makes for the cop as fast as his little goody-two-shoes will carry him.

Raleigh made for the exit. He pulled out with great civility, tried not to run over dead Dennis, got us the living fuck outta there. Down a half a mile, he jumped the median, hauled ass the other direction.

We passed the rest area and Raleigh said, "Look like our boy Dennis officially dead." Meaning the county cop had found him.

I looked over—quiet, but a couple of new truckers looking in the direction of the cop and the deceased. "Man, I hate it for Dennis, but it sure solves a big problem."

"Coming up with four thousand dollars for him?"

"What four thousand dollars? No, him getting vengeful when he figured he'd been punked."

"Wonder why the little motherfucker showed up out here?"

I shrugged. "I'd suspect he was gonna see if he could get a better deal outta Rennie. What I can't figure is why didn't he call Ren, tell on us for putting him in the freezer?"

"Couldn't do it. All these gadgets we got now, nobody worries about remembering phone numbers anymore, bread." Raleigh plucked a phone from a shirt pocket, wiggled his eyebrows. "The man's memory was all right here." He slid his window down, flicked Dennis's phone off into the night. It clicked against the highway and became shrapnel.

"Goddam, you're a frighteningly clever bastard, Raleigh Lightstep."

[12]

Tossed Raleigh out at his hutch, drove the big sled to my crib, hobbled it on the street.

Didn't even go in. Got straight in the Vette, beat tire to Rennie's last known address.

Someone was going to call Rennie if I had to leave the place looking like the Manson clan had dropped by. The unfulfilled adrenaline from the evening's shenanigans had me jerky and knotted up. And I'd fucking had it—some-fucking-body was gonna get me the fuck in front of Rennie like right fucking now.

The closer I got, the more revved I got. Pulled up to the ivied gates at a near-boil, ready for someone to give me some shit and there's Ren's red Ferrari on the pink pavers.

Okay. Cool.

Honk.

The big white kid appears, waves a congenial come-on, uses his gate dingus.

I pull in, park, cross pavers, say: "You gonna wand me tonight?"

He smiled. "No. This way, Mr. Sloan."

Looked like he'd gotten straightened out on my lofty status since last I visited, so I followed his back down the hall by the stair. "The Spanish blood still pissed at me?"

The big kid sniggered. "I bet he is. He got sent out to the fernery. You know how far out in the sticks that is."

I didn't, but why mention it? "For being shitty with me?"

"Some. Being shitty to the lady mostly. She fired him but Rennie's a softy—he just sent him to the boonies."

"Sucks."

The kid agreed, pointed at a door. He used the knob, sent the door back.

I went in and the door clicked behind me.

The room was a combination of library and office. Great mahogany shelves went up ten feet on three sides of the room. A brass rail ran top and bottom; a rolling ladder was affixed to the rails. The shelves were full of books that had that noble, snotty look unread books develop over time. A mahogany desk hardly bigger than a Freightliner nestled in the books. A tall-backed desk chair was turned away from me but I knew Ren was in it.

"You have a nice evening, Ren?"

The chair spun. He looked like shit. His Castilian features and complexion needed a funeral cosmetologist just to look semi-moribund. His dark straight hair was tied back in a rope of ponytail like he'd always worn it. He was thinner than I'd ever seen him, giving his long lanky frame an Ichabod-Crane appearance.

Those three, four years hadn't been kind, but the recent had been worse and it was plastered all over his face. That and a question mark.

"I was there, Ren. I saw your parole guy Dennis fall down."

He was bewildered but he got out: "I'm so fucking glad you're here." Then he put his hands on the desk, lay his head on them and cried quietly.

It was a lonesome sound made of bale and woe and I let him have it out.

I sat in a brocade wingback, watched the top of Rennie's head, thought about nothing. I was afraid if I thought about much at all, I'd get up and slam Rennie's face into his handsome desk a time or two. So I sat, watched a worrisome thumbnail.

In a bit he corralled it, sniffed it up, said, "There's a bar in that closet."

I didn't want to seem rude, so I jumped up, asked Ren what he was drinking. He said he was fine.

I made two three-finger Glenfiddiches with a little ice. I put one in front of Ren, sat back down with mine and sipped it while Rennie blasted his in one gulp. It made his eyes water up.

"Who was shooting at you, Rennie?"

"I have no idea." He fiddled absently with a bauble on a chain around his neck that I recognized. I'd had one like it but had lost it when I was a kid.

"You still got that cheesy St. Chris?"

He looked at it like he was making sure he had it on. "Yeah. You lost yours, didn't you?"

I admitted as much.

He laughed at the piece. "It's a piece of shit but I've held on to it. Don't know why—just have."

I knew why. It represented the comfort of that past Rennie and I shared. It was nothing but a plastic bauble and I envied him for it. It was nothing but the only foothold on a sheer cliff face I'd slid down long ago.

I brought us back to point: "You got enemies?"

"Sloan, I sell dope. Only all the competition is adversarial."

"I didn't say adversarial, Ren."

Rennie shrugged, rose, went in the bar closet. From in there: "Not really." He appeared with another drink, came from a pocket with a pill vial made in the image of a gnome, popped a few, chased them with scotch. "The cultivation crowd is fairly innocuous. For the most part."

"Why don't you make me a list of the part that's not so innocuous? Lemme take a look see. I'll also need addresses and names of your other growers."

"No problem. I'll call and let them know you're coming by."

"Un-un. Don't tell anybody scat. Not yet."

I watched Ren slide a cheek on the corner of the desk, dangle a leg and look like he'd never shed a tear in his life. The oddest sensation bumped me off center: I felt like I was looking at Rennie

Alvarez but I couldn't focus on him somehow. Said: "You been getting threats, anything like that?"

"Un-un. It's been quiet since the night I called you." His bony shoulders apologized with a shrug. "That's why I hadn't called you back."

Bullshit. "Ren, I've been out there working for myself. Being my own fucking client, goddammit. This is *your* shit, not mine. Was *your* parole officer, not mine. Was *your* dead girl in *your* fucking grow house."

"You're right, Sloan, it is *my* shit. Whadda you usually get for something like this?"

"Don't worry about it."

"Un-huh. I can afford. Whadda you get?"

"You wouldn't believe it, Ren. Save your dough."

"Is ten enough for a retainer?"

I'd been working for the wrong people. I'd have been happy with five.

I dead-panned Rennie while he wrote a check and pushed it at me. "Can you start tonight?"

"I think I already did, Ren, but before we go *anywhere* together you're gonna tell my why you've been dodging me."

He wagged his head a bit. "I've been listening to the wrong people."

"Who?"

"They're outta the picture now."

I doubted it. I asked: "Who was the girl in the car, Ren?"

Rennie shrugged. "A girl who worked for me, lived in the house. Hired help—nothing more really."

This was a Rennie Alvarez I didn't know, the one I couldn't focus on.

"Any wild theories on her demise?"

"Nada. She'd worked for me for a couple a years. Seemed like a nice enough person. I've got no idea why anyone would kill her."

He really didn't care.

"You let her family know?" Of course he didn't.

"No. I don't know how to contact them."

"You try?"

He shrugged. "No. How?"

Just for curiosity's sake: "What was her name?"

"Janie, Jane Wall."

I repeated the name internally, said, "Who's here?"

"Iveta and two security people. I've gotta be back at the fernery tonight so I'll take one and leave one here."

"No. You need to get some sleep. You'll be safer here."

"I really need to go. I've got some titrations running in my lab. I've *got* to run out there and read them."

"You've got a lab?" got me a grin.

"State of the art, muchacho. Wanna go see what a nice electron microscope looks like?"

"Tomorrow, Ren." I thought about how I wasn't big on spend-the-night parties, but the situation seemed to dictate such. "I'll camp out here tonight."

He seemed too tired to argue and I was glad. I had questions he'd answer in the morning, but tonight I said, "Get some rest."

"I'll show you where you're sleeping."

"Lemme talk to your boys first, get them set up for the night."

"I'm going on up. Top of the stairs, go right. I'll leave a light on."

"I'm gonna leave the door open and put one a your thugs on the stair—you and the missus behave yourselves."

"Nothing to worry about there, I can assure you. See you in the morning."

I had nothing to say. Rennie got up and left. I made myself one last neat one from his single mead. Took it back to the wingback and sat for a while trying to remember who the fuck I thought I was fooling.

***

The bedroom door clicked shut. I eased over the side of the bed with my piece, lay quietly on the floor.

The bed jiggled.

I stood, pointed my gun, turned on the lamp then snapped the lamp off.

Fingers raked my skivs down and I backed away. "This is too weird, Iveta."

"He is gone. He left for the fernery."

I huffed, said, "You gotta be kidding me."

"Not a problem. I am to take you there tomorrow. He took only one of the security people. The other is asleep on the stairs."

The noise in the room was deafening: it was my breathing. I stood there—I had nothing.

She said, from the darkness, "Please do not embarrass me and send me away."

I was easy. I let my breath go; it slid out between my teeth in a hiss.

She followed my serpent's sound, found me in the dark and I cuckolded my best friend copiously until dawn.

[13]

Woke alone, dressed alone, left alone. In the foyer there was a gadget lying on the low table by the door. The gadget looked as though it might open the front gate. It did so I took it with me, closed the gate after I'd passed through.

Shoulda felt guilty about what I'd left in my rearview, but didn't.

Shoulda been dreading seeing Booker at the Sheriff's office, but somehow I wasn't.

Rennie was a liar so I'd fucked his wife and was ready to give him up to the cops at the slightest provocation.

I didn't know what he was up to and I didn't know what his wife was up to. Somehow it didn't seem like they were playing doubles, but who could know? I did know I was being played. I'd been played before and my play-dar was going like an air-raid siren.

I didn't care. If Booker sat on *me*, I'd dump Rennie's name and address on *him*, that simple.

Sure. That simple. Sure it was. Shoulda been but for a couple of complications. One: God loves irony. Two: God hates me.

***

The new Sheriff's Department building is a former Montgomery Ward store, if that's last week enough for you. The county fertilized it with good old boomtown tax revenue and it grew another four stories or so. Impressive place full of truth and justice, I'm sure.

An unfriendly young lady behind some thick glass looked at her computer like it was a great inconvenience. Said: "No."

I said: "Whadda you mean: *no*?"

"*No*, you're not on the appointment list." Seemed responding had become inconvenient too.

"Wait. I gotta have an appointment to see a detective?"

"Un-huh."

I gave up, asked could she call Booker. She did, but it looked like she wanted to charge extra for it. It got me past security anyhow.

I had divested myself of all firearms, knives, knucks-o-brass, and explosive devices earlier in the car so I squeaked by but only because the scofflaw detector was out for calibration.

Took an elevator up to the third floor as advised by the hard working girl at the front desk. Rode upwards with some people you'd expect to find at a modern cop-house but—looking around me—it seemed it was getting harder to tell the good guys from the bad guys.

My floor opened up and no one but me got off.

A perky girl who had to be an intern or something sat at a desk that was an obvious obstacle between me and the detectives behind her. Looked like fessing up to a major crime in this county had become a lotta goddam trouble. They just didn't do walk-ins anymore I guessed. I said: "Booker."

She worked a keypad, spoke quietly into a handset, laughed, lay the phone down. Whatever Booker had said made her look at me funny. She didn't share; she said, "There's a waiting area about halfway back, on your right, Mr. Sloan. Glass front, couple of couches, vending machines. You can't miss it. You are Mr. Sloan, right?"

I admitted it, thanked her, walked around the desk, through an open area of desks full of detectives. Each and every one looked up at me, knew instantly and collectively that I wasn't on their team. I smiled back anyway and moved into a long hall.

The earlier mentioned waiting room was where it was supposed to be and fit the description. A woman of maybe sixty-five and a couple of kids watched Drew try to be Bob on a TV mounted high on a wall. A pretty dumb-looking man on the TV with Drew had guessed a pack of popcorn was eight bucks and we all watched a cardboard skier yodel his ass over the cliff. Everyone in the audience ah-ed their sympathy for the dumb guy. No one in the waiting room seemed to care.

The kids were about ten and twelve it looked like. The younger picked up an electronic dingus and made it jingle. The older kid nabbed it in one swift swipe.

The younger kid protested. "Gramma, Trevor yanked the DS outta my hand."

The gramma looked from the TV. "Trevor, why are you being mean to your brother?"

Trevor shrugged out some dunno, tossed the gadget at his brother. The granny went back to *The Price Is Right*. Little brother fired the game up. Trevor and I watched each other while I found a seat across the room on the other couch.

Booker came by, stuck his head in, smiled at the granny, said, "Miz Wall, I'll talk to you and the boys in just a minute."

He had another smile for me he'd probably been saving awhile. He put it on me, said, "Enjoy the wait, Sloan."

I felt the blood gush and I'm sure I either blanched or blushed. It was so obvious the name Wall had registered with me that Booker nodded, put some more grin on it. He said, "Was you gone tell me?"

I said, "Yeah. I found out last night."

He watched me for a few seconds trying to see if I exhibited any signs of lying.

He kept his eyes on me, but said, "Miz Wall, this the private fella I was tellin you about, the one knows the man your daughter worked for."

Said it just like that, walked the fuck out.

***

Was the little guy started it. The rest of us sat there sorta stunned.

"You know who it was killed our mom?"

"No."

The other kid, Trevor, the older one, jumped in. "Aren't you s'posed to be some kinda big-shot private detective?"

"No. I'm not a big deal." I wasn't even a private eye in any legal sense.

The older kid said, "See, Gramma, I told you he wasn't gonna be any help. Nobody is. Nobody cares."

Gramma hushed Trevor, looked at me with weary, begging eyes. Her eyes wrote me a book. They said she was treading water, a kid under each arm. Said she didn't have time to give a damn who'd killed her daughter. But the eyes said it mattered to Janie Wall's sons.

The little kid asked, "Do you care, mister?"

I asked, "What's your name?"

"Felix."

"Yes, Felix, I care. Now that I've met you and your brother and your gramma, I care even more."

Felix was sold. Trevor rolled his eyes, picked up the Nintendo.

[14]

"Pretty funny shit, Booker. Thanks."

"Hmmm. You think that shit's funny, watch your face now. Dennis Toussaint."

At this point in my day—considering it started at Rennie's a little after midnight, interrupted only by two, three hours of restless, guilt-ridden sleep—I'm well beyond any oh-my moments. Couple of motherless children pretty much finish knocking off the high points, leave the lows looking like canyons.

We're in Booker's office and I'm having no fun, but like I say: this point, it's just another link in a sad chain of events called today. Looking stupid was easy so I talked stupid too. "Who?"

"Dennis Two-saint. Don't tell me you ain't heard of him. Got hisself dead at a rest area on the Four, out Tampa way."

"Happens. Why do I care?"

"I didn't suspect you would but then I got this case, this parole fella who got hisself dead. So bout six this mornin—couldn't sleep so I come in early—I'm lookin at the folder, see. Next thing you know, I open this Toussaint fella's call log. Guess who's on it? Go on, Sloan, guess."

I guessed Paul Reubens and I was wrong.

"Was your buddy Raleigh Lightstep. So I go: *Hmm, didn't Sloan say sump'n bout his boy bein paroled out to Seminole County?* I call Raleigh when his shift started this mornin and guess what? He's takin a few days sick leave." I got a smile full of happy.

"It's only a matter a time, Sloan, fore I get this motherfucker. I get to him fore you show up with him, it's gone go bad for you and him both. Dig?"

I was getting bored. Being the *piñata* at a Booker party gets old. He's jovial and almost genteel—almost—but it gets tedious as watching Sumo.

So I go: "You guys find the Wackenhut guy in the weeds yet?"

Booker glares, says: "Say how."

"Couple in the back, one in the head. Three guys gift-wrapped him, tossed him over the fence."

"You see it?"

"On or off the record?"

"Know who did it?"

"Not yet, Booker."

Booker watched me a long minute and a half. He said, "I'll see can I find this Wackenhut boy's wife and young'uns, bring 'em in let you meet 'em."

I told him I was good, told him I had all the motivation I could stand for a day. Told him Rennie's name and address.

Told him how Raleigh and I ended up at the rest area. He thought the Dennis-in-the-freezer part was pretty funny shit.

I didn't tell him about impersonating a Federal agent, fucking Rennie's wife or about the fernery where Rennie was laying dogo. Nor about breaking into a state facility or abusing Raleigh's ex's house while she was abroad corporating.

I asked how he found the grandmother and the kids. He said they found him after they found the girl in the morgue.

"Wish you coulda been there for that, Sloan, sure do wish you coulda been there. The gran'mamma come out, say, yeah, it's her daughter. See, I don't know why, but she had them two young'uns with her. They was with me out'n the hall. The oldest boy, he just stood there, but the littlest'un, he go to screamin. Wish you coulda seen it."

Passed on playing it clever, said, "We done here?"

"Yeah, I guess." He looked at a pad on his desk. He'd been scribbling on it as we talked. "Your boy gone be at this address here?"

"I doubt it." Truth.

"You know where he is?"

"Un-un. He slipped off last night after we talked." Near lie.

"You still sure it wasn't him killed this Wall girl?"

"I'm hoping, Booker." Truth.

We watched each other a while.

I broke first. "Look, Booker, my ass is on the line here. I got Raleigh's ass on the line. If my friend Rennie's clean, then his ass is on the line. Now there's those two kids and their granny, thank you very much."

"And don't forget about me. I'm crawled bout halfway up your ass on this thing my-own-self. We need some action, Sloan. I'm lettin you walk outta here now, but next time I see you, if you ain't got me somebody to take to Thirty-Third Street jail, then I'm takin you. Dig?"

Dig. I got up and walked.

***

I did dig.

The sad part? Besides her kids and her mom, nobody cared if Janie Wall died or went the fuck to El Paso.

So I had to go and care. But only because I'm a fucking chump, see? Warmhearted, soft-in-the-head, lead-with-your-chin Sloan. They should save a special parking spot down at Publix: *Chump of the Month Parking Only*. I could be a persistent contender.

I was pissed, confused, frustrated and pretty bothered. I was sure that going to Ren's fernery and royally kicking his ass would help more than anything else that would come to mind. The new Rennie: Rennie the sociopath. Janie Wall was no more than furniture to him. Worked for him for two years and he says she seemed like a nice enough person for a nobody bud trimmer.

Something had changed or died or was terribly broken with this new Rennie. I didn't know who he was, wasn't sure he did.

Drove back to Rennie's far too fast and too aggressive. Used my gate opener on the gate. No one complained. Used the butt of my Nine on the front door glass when no one answered my chimes or knocks or banging.

The big white kid's feet and legs showed on the stair.

I said, "You clear my line of sight with one of those nancy grease guns, I'll kneecap you, both legs. You hear me, kid?"

He must have—he stopped.

"I said do you hear me?"

"Yeah."

"Good. I'm coming up to talk to the lady."

"She's still asleep."

"I doubt it. You wanna lay the piece on the stair or you want I should kneecap you?"

He cursed but dropped his hardware. "You keep making me look like shit, dude."

"Yeah, I know, and I'm sorry as hell. Why don't you come on down?"

More cursing and a handgun hit the carpeted stair next to the burper. Sneaky fuck.

He came down, hands halfheartedly out at his side. He was again very disappointed in himself.

As he went by, he asked, "You gonna shoot me if I make coffee?"

"Be my guest."

"She's back in her bedroom." He gave me a conspirator's face, telling me he was smart enough to know she'd been in my bedroom and why.

I told him to mind his manners, and don't forget to get his toys off the stairs after I was gone.

It took a couple of doors to find the right one. Iveta pretended to sleep; a leg, an arm and a breast were painfully white where they'd escaped cover.

I said, "I'm not fucking you."

She rustled, snuggled in, said, "Yes you are."

"No. You're taking me to the fernery. Now. Get up."

"Fuck me." She stretched, flipped the bedding back, gave me the sleepy eyes.

"No. I'm not fucking you." But only because fucking her would render kicking Ren's ass totally inappropriate.

"Yes, you are."

I gave it one last valiant, *No, I'm not*, and then fucked her like I hated her. She fucked me back, guttural sounds coming from her that were never meant to emanate from something that lovely.

The end was violent and physical. After her body finished pushing back, she slapped me a time or two, told me she hated me. Told me to get the hell off her and leave.

I stayed in character, rolled off, pimp cool. Rolled to my knees, grabbed her hair, pulled her up to a sitting position, tilted her head back so I could look in her face.

"Get your clothes on. You're taking me to the fernery, remember?"

Iveta made some lioness sounds deep in her throat, nestled into me. "No. Is no fun there. Is more fun here, Duncan."

I turned her hair loose, bent her head forward and kissed her neck. "Playtime's over. Go get dressed, sweetie."

She flopped her pretty head back in my face again. "And I was only just getting... How do you say it?"

"Warmed up?"

"No, Duncan Sloan, I am beyond warmed up."

"Go. Clothes, shoes."

[15]

The road to De Leon Springs did a two-lane twist through some pretty forgotten Florida. Iveta put the big Mercedes to task with a nice, easy touch. It was a pleasure to witness.

While I watched, she said, "What shall we do?"

"About what?" I knew *what*—I was buying time, maybe hoping she'd forget.

"Us. Last night, this morning."

"I truly don't know, Iveta."

"I do not love him, Sloan. I am not sure I even like him."

"None of that matters. You're married to him."

"So, we are done?"

"No. I just don't know what happens next. You're the wife of a friend."

"What if he does not care?"

"I do."

"So now you find your scruples."

I looked over, showed her my face.

"Sorry. That was unfair."

No, it wasn't but my bully ego accepted the apology no matter. "Thank you. I'll think on how to go about it."

"Ask him."

"What?"

"If he cares."

I couldn't think of any diplomatic way to go to Rennie and breech that fortification. I wasn't sure it mattered. Wasn't sure Iveta and I *weren't* done.

Sat back, watched the road unwind, tried to remember exactly when I forgot to remember: *Never fuck the client; the client's wife is the client too.*

The car slowed, found a wide drive through an open gate.

Iveta dropped the landing gear and planted the steel under some ancient live oak trees.

She slid the selector to *park* and placed the selecting hand on my hand.

"Let me find Rennie. He is probably in his la-bora-tory." Said it like Zsa Zsa would've. "Look around. This is the legitimate portion of our little domain." Back to Lady-of-the-Manor.

I got out, stretched every voluntary muscle I was intimate with a couple of times, checked out this fernery Rennie had himself.

Seemed indeed legit and worked by Mexican labor. Other than the perennial sketchiness of using Mexicans due to the convincing counterfeit paperwork available now, I could see only law abiding ferns and ornamentals.

A big white house with lap-siding needed a paint job about the time video killed the radio star and was still wanting. A high, wide porch wrapped around three sides. You couldn't have put a soda bottle on the porch for the detritus. Boxes and crates and machinery I'd never seen. Pots, buckets, broken shit, sundry tools in various states of disrepair. Only a narrow path was free—it led to a door.

There were two shabby, but newer, lower houses off to the left. Brown women watched from porches as brown children played with dirt.

Off to the right were six greenhouses you could have played tennis in. Everywhere outside were fern beds and ornamentals in plastic buckets boxed off with railroad ties. Laborers toiled in them.

I looked back at the house, looked up over the porch. The Latino kid from Rennie's was in a window giving me some serious stink-eye.

A compadre walked up behind him so I blew them both a kiss.

The compadre thought it was funny.

I lost interest, turned toward the flora.

"¿Donde esta Senior Alvarez?"

A tiny man with a square head and a large hat pointed to the greenhouses.

I said, "*Gracias, gracias.*"

He said, nice south Texas drawl in it, "He's in back, in the last'n on your right, pardner."

It made us both grin.

"Thanks, Tex."

He tipped his hat, went back to stooping among the plants. I wandered on, thinking how a more centered and connected individual could have found solace and self, zenned the fuck out among the lush flora. Just looked like commerce to me since I don't know a rutabaga from a begonia.

The tall yellow-toned kid from Rennie's was perched on a tall stool by a high tool-rack attached to the last greenhouse. I didn't see a gat but I was sure there would be one skulking around under his baggy attire.

My presence seemed to amuse him. "S'up, Tio?"

"Nada, Sambo. Where's the boss?"

I bumped a set of inviting knucks.

The kid's other hand jerked over a shoulder. "I'd give it a minute if I was you."

Hard voices came from inside the greenhouse but tall lush plant life guarded the arguers from my prying eyes.

"What's your real name, kid?"

"What if I said it really was Sambo?"

"I'd say your parents hated you."

He said, "Or had a crazy-wicked sense of humor. Nate."

The tool rack became a door, swung back on hinges. Iveta came through the void; I could see Ren over her shoulder.

"I told him we fucked like minks after he left."

I looked from a retreating Iveta to Rennie. All he had was embarrassment. Me too.

***

Rennie's lab bore more semblance to a horrible collision involving a frat-house kitchen and a Pyrex delivery truck than it did to a place for doing R&D on extreme *mota*-cultivating. Really it bore more semblance to Ren's life than anything else—a total fucking mess.

He says: "Don't worry about it, Sloan."

"But I am worrying about it."

"I'm not."

"Rennie, goddammit, stop titrating or what-the-fuck-ever you're doing and talk to me."

Ren had a long glass tube I remembered from chem lab between a thumb and finger, another finger over one of the open ends. He pointed the other end into a beaker, released his finger—green goo flowed into the beaker. He lay the glass tube down, swirled the beaker's contents. My brain clicked over a notch and, for no particular reason, my sketchy education found: *pipette.*

"Ren, stop it, look at me."

He huffed, put the beaker on the stainless steel table.

"Get over it. Sloan, I don't care if you fucked my wife."

I had to ask: "Why not?"

"Because I don't." He took off his glasses, wiped the bridge of his nose then his eyes with a wad of paper towel. He lay the glasses down, qualified with a shrug, said, "And I don't know why. I don't care for sex one way or another. Never really have, I guess." More shrug. "Never really got into it as a kid. Don't worry about it."

I wouldn't be let off that easy. "Ren, I'm your friend. I fucked your wife. You gotta be pissed. Please be pissed. Come on."

Nada.

"Ren, you gotta say something here." I put my hands out like some slacker Christ.

All I got from him: "I'm glad it was you and I'm sure she was grateful."

I'm stunned. I want the fucker to punch me, throw deadly chemicals in my face, something, anything. I get nada.

Okay. So I say, "Un-huh. You're welcome, Ren. She was totally responsive. You could see she'd been neglected. Glad I could help."

I watched his eyes. They weren't the same eyes I'd always known and Rennie knew what I saw. The moment went awkward; I said: "You got all these punks with expensive weapons, big time cat like you, why'd you call me Ren? Why didn't you call in a gunsel or two to clean up?"

It read out: the new look on Rennie was a flickering vacancy sign. He shrugs again, says, "They weren't around then. They're new."

"Where'd they come from, Ren?"

He watched the beaker, spoke to me. "A referral from someone in the club. They're an outfit that specializes in, uh..." He went lame.

"I get it." I watched him watch the beaker, said, "You're pulling something on me, dog. I don't know what and I don't know why. You wanna share?"

"Why would I pull something on you? You're my oldest friend." So what does the dickhead do? He goes back to his glassworks.

"You get me that list of the assholes in your life?"

He wiped his hands on his lab coat, fished a bent piece of paper from a big pocket, pushed it at me with a smile. "All my locations of business, all my competition that could care enough to be dangerous."

I said *thanks*, turned to go, knowing my back would get spoken to.

Rennie said, "Go easy, brother. She's not who you think she is."

I didn't look back then, but when I look back now, I wonder why the dumb-fuck didn't listen to his own advice.

[16]

I'd had quite enough of the Alvarez clan, so Jesus, or someone as philanthropic as he, had made sure the keys were in Iveta's Teutonic sleigh.

Stole the car. Drove it like I'd stolen it. I pushed enough *open* buttons on enough remote operating gadgets to throw Rennie's ivied gates into hasty retreat. Also got a couple of garage doors moving as well as the big white-boy gunsel. Dropped the for-show ride like a bad habit on the pretty pavers that lapped at Rennie's sublime digs.

When I had sole on paver, I tossed White-Boy Iveta's keys. I didn't say shit—had about nada to say to any of the branches of the Rennie tree. Just bent my frame enough to fall into my old mother ship, charged the starter, fed the carb, pushed the shifter into first.

Watched the punk working a phone while I circled around and hit the street of intoleration out front that led to fresh air. The signs strategically placed by Rennie's mini-burg thanked me for leaving. I slid the windows down, let the stench out.

My Lincoln was still on the curb in front of my pad. One too many cars for one man and so many poor desperate souls in need of transportation.

I went inside, got the Lincoln's keys, walked them out and stuck them in the ignition.

Don't say I never do my part to fight poverty and desperation. Come, take my sins away. Please. Drive them to the church or synagogue of your choice.

On a whim, a fucking whim, I reach in and pop the Lincoln's trunk, right? Wanted to see if Uncle Raleigh had left any surface-to-air shit back there. I walked around, took a look.

My my—nice rush.

My my. There you go, now. Guys I barely knew, stacked in there like cordwood.

I eased the trunk down. It clicked and my nipples got hard and my knees got squeaky. I stepped away.

Cell: Raleigh.

"Hey..."

"Got a trunk-full a trouble."

Quiet like a capital *Q* with a capital *T*.

"Where're you and your trouble?"

"My crib."

"You wanna talk about it?"

"Un-un, like big I don't wanna talk, baby. How about you just head this way?"

"See you in a minute." And gone like a local fad.

***

I was still out front watching the Lincoln to make sure it behaved itself when Raleigh rolled in. I tossed him the Lincoln's keys, inviting him to take a look while I got Windex and paper towels.

We invested a good half-hour wiping down the inside of the car and arguing about damage control.

Raleigh had some Machiavellian shit that could have involved a good deal of both driving and digging. I was for leaving the sled in crack town with the key in it. Crack town is never far away anymore no matter where you live, and, face it, my way involved very little physical or mental investment. Machiavelli lost out to Alley Oop.

Nothing but a little more illegal and improper disposal of a body times three. Went off hitchless; Raleigh scooped me and we exited the hood.

I found the fold of paper Ren had passed me. Unfolded it.

The info didn't move me. The locales were predictable, the names, predictably, rang no bells.

I re-folded it, put it away, watched the window.

"Where you at, Sloan?"

"I'm thinking Rennie's operation's tight as a sieve. I tell him last night about being at the scene of the crime and today I got dead people out in front of my house."

"Starting to look like somebody don't like you."

"Or somebody's sending sign language."

"What's that mean?"

"You look at those motherfuckers?"

"Not much—I seen dead people before."

"You didn't notice they were dressed a lot like the three guys who were shooting at Rennie?"

Raleigh chewed that a bit, said, "You get scared and drop out, you gone still owe me extra."

"Raleigh, Dennis may have hung up on you, but some bold motherfuckers left three stiffs on my doorsteps."

"Which means what?"

"I'm gonna find out who the fuck did it, talk to 'em about it, whoever the fuck it was."

"That's my baby Sloan. Don't fuck up and get shot."

"You know me—I always try not to."

We rode on in some fairly serious quiet for an uncomfortable few.

Raleigh said it for us. Said: "We neck-deep in this shit now, Sloan."

I said, "I *been* neck-deep in it, dog." But didn't mention Trevor and Felix Wall.

"Where we going?"

It was about two o'clock, time to put some knuckles on some doors. I looked at Rennie's fact sheet, read off an address. "Know it?"

Raleigh admitted he could get us close with his GPS.

I dared him to prove it, so he did.

Put us on a spot coulda been related to Raleigh's ex's digs but for the no-lake. Stucco, barrel tile, St. Augustine and floral friends. The occupant, according to Rennie's list, was a Pat—no gender offered.

Raleigh dropped us on the driveway and no one decided to answer our front door knocks. Nor at the rear slider.

We, as in I, yanked the slider open with little effort.

Found the occupant hiding in the laundry room. It was a she and she asked rather earnestly that Raleigh and I not kill her, so we didn't. We just moved into the kitchen and the skunk smell of krypie.

She was a heavy, serious-faced young woman, maybe thirty. Her clothes were casual and loose, stained here and there with evidence of her agricultural profession.

I asked: "Why would we kill you?"

"They killed Janie."

Fine conversation until I asked who *they* were.

She clammed.

"Pat, we're working for Rennie."

It got her thinking.

I pressed. "We're looking for *they*. Gonna find 'em too."

She checked me out, appraised Raleigh, said, "Good luck when you do."

Pat and I watched the other's eyes. I said, "You're not gonna help us, are you?"

She shook her mousey mop. "No."

"They that scary?"

The mop nods. "Yes."

I eyed Raleigh—he shrugged.

"You have a change of heart, call. But don't wait till someone's putting two in your forehead like they did Janie—I'm not that fast." I held a business card out there.

We watched eyes again. She let the card hang.

I broke first, grinned, shrugged, wished her good luck as well, put my card away.

***

An electronic sentry demanded numbers. I fed the ones on Rennie's fact sheet to Raleigh, he fed them to the gadget. The gadget gave the okay and a jerky iron gate conceded a nice hood out in the super-burbs.

Once again no one answered our beck at the front entry. Once again I tricked a slider into opening. Somebody really should do something about sliding-glass-door security.

Found this urban farmer, a cat named Gene, upstairs strupping a young girl who might have been driving age. Or not.

I suggested to the girl that she get dressed while Gene asked us not to kill them.

Raleigh said, "Damn, Sloan, these folks all think every motherfucker breaks in gonna kill 'em." Then to Gene: "Why you think we gonna kill you? Cause a Janie?"

Gene wasn't keeping up well and the girl's young white skin flashing around wasn't helping anybody. He managed a weak nod.

Everything about Gene was pretty weak: weak chin, weak hairline, weak eyes. Yeah, Gene looked a lot like somebody who wouldn't mind knocking off a shot of jail-bait now and again.

I told the girl: "You need to grab your clothes and beat it, honey, like right now."

She gave me a nice, respectful *yessir* and scooted.

"Talk to us, Gene."

"Who are ya'll?" He was sitting up, covering his pride with an unlaundered sheet.

"Hired help. Rennie's."

The relief was obvious but was probably what led to a bad judgment call. "Then ya'll can go fuck ya'selves."

Oh my.

Raleigh began as a blur in my peripheral view. He materialized instantly in Gene's shit. Yanked naked Gene up and simultaneously popped him a couple of good ones in and around the head. "You better spill some beans, motherfucker, or I'll slap you into the middle of next week."

Gene held tight.

Raleigh practiced his best one-hand bitch-slap.

Gene no yakky.

Raleigh looks at me.

I shrug. "All I saw was a side-by-side if you're having fantasies about putting him in a freezer."

"This shit keeps getting harder and harder, bread."

I agreed but didn't mention it. I said, "Gene, I don't know how they scared you and Pat, but I gotta hand it to 'em. What I wanna know is: are they looking to take a cut or looking to take over?"

Gene watched me a long moment, said, "I'd say they want it all." He pulled himself free of Raleigh, sat on the bed. "And that's all I'm saying." Shook his head, covered himself again. Said: "Ya'll can beat me unconscious, and that's all I'm saying."

[17]

Raleigh backed about halfway down Gene's drive, stopped, said, "Fear and pain're powerful persuaders."

We were debating the merits of tuning Gene up a bit more. I jerked a thumb and Raleigh backed on out.

"So is greed. He'd a hucked us. Gene's a cockroach. Guarantee he's got his own agenda in this deal. See can you circle around the block here."

"Ain't you got a list of places?"

"Yeah, but I got faith in Gene. Don't you?"

"He does seem like a motherfucker would have an agenda if that counts for anything."

Raleigh eased around a street or two leisurely enough we nearly missed Gene's exit scene. It was neither leisurely nor pretty.

Gene came out of his drive, missed the apron two feet on the passenger side. He was in an older Jag sedan and it jostled stiffly when he bounced over the curb.

Raleigh fell in behind, kept his distance. A car was in front of Gene at the automatic gate and it made Gene impatient. The gate opened and Gene and the car in front went through nearly as one. Raleigh slid through, backed off.

Gene hit the main road, a two-lane blacktop, passed the lead car on a double yellow and got smaller.

I gave Raleigh some eyebrows. He told me I shoulda drove if I was gonna feel the need to supervise.

The road gained a center turn lane and Raleigh used it like an HOV lane. We caught Gene at a stop sign a mile down the road. The three-lane fell into a four-lane that fell into an interstate highway and we were headed back toward downtown. Then we were beyond downtown and its absurdly fresh skyline.

Off-ramp. Left. Left. Right into a declining strip mall.

Raleigh held up and we watched Gene roll by a women's shop, a counterfeit perfume shop, a Latino market, a couple of vacant units then toss the Jag in a slot.

He sat. We sat.

Maybe fifteen minutes, a middle-aged guy came from one of the unoccupied units. He had a thin moustache that went down around his mouth and matching thin sideburns. Print shirt, cheap slacks, those silly shoes with the long duckbill toes.

He cleared his sinuses and expressed the residue onto the landscaping. Found a cigarette, puff-puff, found sunglasses, walked to Gene's Jag like regular folk.

Less than ten he's out of Gene's Jag, new cig, same old tacky shades. He crossed the traffic lane to the sidewalk while Gene ignited the Jag and backed out.

Raleigh fired up as well. "Who we looking at?"

"We know where Gene lives."

"I hear you. Ain't no rides out here match our boy. I'm gone pull around back, see do they got shop-owner parking back there."

Raleigh put us where we could see a big burgundy Cadillac SUV where Sideburn's back door should have been. We had a couple of nonsensical arguments over nothing to pass time and our new friend was rolling.

He backed out, came at us.

Raleigh and I slumped.

The Caddy-in-a-box passed. It was heavily tinted, but I could see a hatchet-face sucking on a cig. Sideburns galore. Cold blue eyes.

He didn't seem to see us but that could just mean he was good.

Sideburns evaporated and Raleigh yanked the car around.

The guy drove conscientiously. So much so that I could only imagine him either oblivious or totally aware we were behind him. If he was aware then he either thought we were stupid or simply didn't care if he was being tailed—and, honestly, there was nothing good about the latter.

The slow escape led us around and up and down some, but in as straight a line as our maniacal map allows, to another strip mall, this one way south of city hall and nearly new.

There was an Ace Hardware and I told Raleigh I wouldn't mind looking, see did Ace have any pump handles.

Raleigh didn't ask—he pulled in a slot near the hardware emporium. Sideburns had to use a key to get in a unit that for all visual info was vacant but for some pretty fancy hieroglyphics painted in red on the storefront glass. There was plain brown painter's paper to discourage the curious, which I was.

"Can you get a fix on his tag?"

"In like fifteen, but it'll cost you."

"What doesn't. Make the call."

"You don't even want to know what the toll is?"

"No. I'll give you fifteen hundred. That's a C a minute."

Raleigh ciphered, nodded, made a call or two.

He put his phone away with such dramatic subtlety I knew it would be good. He dead-panned me his best dead-pan, said, "Iveta Alvarez."

I would've furrowed up and said *un-un*, but my head noodles were like crazy snakes looking for how that shit made an iota of sense.

Couldn't make it work so I furrowed up, said, "Un-un."

"Fuck, Sloan, I'm gone take you by Walgreens, let you get a spiral notebook so you can keep up with all these change-outs and switch-backs."

My phone does calisthenics opening and closing calling Ren and Iveta, getting the neither. I left shitty messages, both posts—so what I stole their car?

Ten minutes, we see three separate sets of sideburns use keys on the door, see one real old set come out. He don't key no lock, saying someone locked behind him, saying he's probably an elder of the What-the-Fuck club these guys were in.

A long and dark car appears magically, scoops *long-temps*, eases into what's morphing into an interesting evening.

Raleigh, ever vigilant, says, "Wanna see where Pee-Paw lives?"

"I'd love to just to have something to write in a spiral notebook, but I wanna stick on the Escalade. If Gene hadn't jumped so fucking quick, we coulda grabbed another car."

The banter fell moot: Sideburns showed with a woman who was either an off-duty titty-dancer or was doing Halloween early as an off-duty titty-dancer.

Sideburns sauntered her to his Caddy box, rubbed the back of her Daisy-Duke's a time or so. He opened the passenger door chivalrously; the tit shaker got in. Then she disappeared.

Sideburns stood in the vee of the partially-open door, hands high, one on the top of the vehicle, the other on top of the door.

Raleigh asked: "The fuck's he doing?"

"I believe he's getting his knob polished, Raleigh."

"That's what I was thinking."

Little quiet, Raleigh says: "Seem kinda seedy, sitting here watching this shit."

"Putting 'em in the freezer, watching 'em get a blow job—all pays the same, dad."

"Ain't nuthin but a thang, huh?"

"Nuthin but a thang."

Sideburns shivered it out, swayed a bit, then—get this—looks around to see who's watching. I mean, wouldn't you look around before if you cared? Afterward is like you're taking bows or something.

The guy pulled his princess out, stuffed what had to be money in her bra, patted her ass and watched it go.

The girl wiggled to a Mustang parked a few slots over, turned, said something. Sideburns looked annoyed, flapped a hand at her, turned back to the Caddy.

The Kewpie pulled the cash from her bra, kissed it then flipped-off Sideburns's back. She slid in the Mustang, melted away.

I laughed, said, "Nice pragmatic young lady right there."

Raleigh thought she had a good sense of humor.

I figured you're a whore, you better have a good sense of humor.

[18]

Sideburns retreated behind the brown paper and I went into the hardware store, not for pump handles but for info on goings-on next door.

I didn't like what I was taking back with me but didn't have time to fuss over it much. There was a youngish sideburner standing by Raleigh's car. He was eager to fold his coat back and show me a complex looking handgun he was holding in his other hand.

Poor chump. I said, "You point that thing at me you'll regret the shit out of it."

I amused him. "Are you quite sure?" Good English, thick delivery. He flapped his coattail back, hid the gat.

Oh my. "Un-huh." I stopped about twenty feet from him. "Cause my man there driving the car'll shoot you in the stomach if you do."

"You think so?"

The original Sideburns came from the glass door, tossed me a little wave and a grin. I said, "I know so." Watched Sideburns load into Iveta's Caddy box and glide.

Junior said, "How, my friend? This is *his* gun."

I put out pleading, beseeching, begging hands, said, "Hey, I'm just saying..."

Junior smiled at my silliness, went dramatic with: "And I'm just saying..." added a nice smooth firearm-brandishing move as he brought the gun from under his jacket.

Raleigh shot him in the stomach.

The guy stumbled back and went on his ass. His face was the shape of a question mark. He looked at Raleigh's pistol in his hand, looked at Raleigh, looked at me. The gat clattered on the asphalt and Junior fell over and began groaning.

Raleigh said, "Hey, Sloan, get my piece, will you?"

I picked up the gun, handed it to Raleigh and a guy came from the storefront. He asked was the kid dead.

I told him not yet and Raleigh and I got the fuck outta Dodge.

***

Raleigh: "Un-un."

Me: "Un-huh."

Pause.

Raleigh: "Un-un."

"Un-huh. Said it was some sorta Serbian club or some kinda Eastern European outfit." That was the dope I got from an old-timer working in the hardware store.

Then Raleigh pulls a *Raleigh*.

You start thinking how full of shit Raleigh is with all his fine wining and dining and faux-culturey crap and artsy-fartsy crap. Then he says something like: "Yep, that's what I thought. Was the Cyrillic alphabet on the window, wasn't it?"

See how he can totally startle you? So I go: "Silly who?"

"Cyrillic. Named after a cat name a Cyril, the patron saint of the Slavs."

"And the Belarusians too?" I'm betting.

"Un-huh. Them too, baby."

Oh my.

I'm riding along over here trying to partition off the bigger pieces of this shit; Raleigh's over there, driving along, dying for me to ask him how he knows the saint who wrote on the window of the Bohunk Club.

Nothing lined up and nothing made sense and nothing would get in a box and stay there. Nothing meant shit but the look on those two kids' faces. Fuck Granny Wall—I don't flinch much over adult angst. As a rule, at some point you coulda done something different to avoid your current dilemma—like me now. Coulda told Ren to go fuck himself; Granny coulda done a better job of child-rearing with Janie maybe. Boo-fucking-hoo for both of us.

And Booker? He was a dick. He set me up, put those fucking brats in front of me, made me give a big goddam and I didn't like it. I like to find my own guilty motivations. Always been good at it—don't need help.

"How the fuck do you know that shit?"

"I invested in some pre-war biblical texts one time. The shit was written in..." It took Raleigh a couple of goes, but he got it out. "...Glagolitic script. Precursor to what your man's clubhouse sign is in: Cyrillic."

See? Faux or pro? I tend to believe *pro*, but treat him like he's *faux* only to keep his ego checked. If he suspected as much, he'd illustrate my passive bigotry in no uncertain terms. Such is our totally fucked up not-friendship.

Raleigh wanted to know what I was thinking.

"You don't wanna know. Throw me out at the house."

"You gone go fuck the girl?" Telling me he'd somehow caught on to the action between Iveta and me.

"Actually, I thought I'd go hide in the bushes and watch her."

"And I'm doing what, bread?"

"Maybe you could practice up not letting Slavic punks take your lunch money."

We rode on and let Raleigh's mouth flinch and make silent false starts.

I shifted around so I could either get out of the car quickly or pull my piece. It was that fucking quiet.

Raleigh made noise, possibly a chuckle. Never heard the man laugh. Known him for years, never heard a single ha-ha.

The chuckle went to a decent laugh I didn't think Raleigh had in him.

Either the laugh was infectious or just funny. Whatever—I laughed.

Raleigh says: "The punk motherfucker stuck a Bic lighter in my neck, took my shit." More laugh. "A motherfucking Bic lighter. I saw that's how he done it, I decided I was gonna bust his ass. Good for him you suggested I shoot him in the stomach."

I was enjoying it way too much. "A lighter?"

"Hey, they was a city cop behind your ass right up till I shot the fuck. You didn't even see the cop, did you?"

I admitted I didn't.

"Yeah, the cop pulls out, that's when the punk braced you."

"And also when you popped him."

"Somebody'd neglected his gun safety training. He kept pushing the clip release, thinking it was the safety."

"So he wasn't even close?"

"Fuck close. Can't nobody shoot my shit but me." Raleigh's left-handed: he held up a bejeweled left hand. "Magic ring, dog. He wasn't throwing shit."

"How terribly modern. Designer handguns." I shuffled in a pocket, had paper. I held it up between a couple of vagrant fingers. "Here's Ren's empire, you wanna take a tour, talk to his subjects."

"Renaldo a little superior?"

"Looking more and more like he grew up to be your typical Cuban-American, harboring that annoying post-Colombian attitude." I smiled for Raleigh over the fancy words.

"Unpack that for me."

"*You know me, you owe me.* Enslaving the locals, pressing severe religions on them, totally disenfranchising them, fun-stuff like that."

"Hmm. Sounds goddam familiar. That where ya'll got that shit?" Going down big-B black.

What? I'm saying what? Wasn't anybody in the car didn't know who *ya'll* was.

[19]

Slid the Shark toward Ren's main digs. Figured no way Iveta was still at the fernery, figured I'd see what went on when I wasn't around.

Tussled with myself until I admitted maybe I wanted to see where Sideburns fit, see if he'd drop by. Put my plastic car on a shoulder, under a tree, maybe three hundred yards from Rennie's front gate. The day, suffering its mortality, was splashing long shadows across the road. I got comfortable, put some decent music on the box.

Maybe fifteen whole minutes, I'm thinking how badly I dislike the surveillance part of this sport. Twenty, my childish attention span is spasming, tugging at the tethers. I said *fuck-it*, pulled away from my hidey spot, glance over at Ren's as I go by.

The fucker's Caddy's in the driveway. Been there at least as long as I had.

I slam the brake, eat some grassy shoulder, let some traffic around. Backed up, used my gate opener, pulled next to the Escalade.

The tall kid Nate greeted me, asked me in, called me *tio.* I called him *Sambo* and we laughed. I wisely suggested we exchange cell digits. Nate cogged on it, agreed it sounded like a good idea and we swapped numbers.

Someone had swept up the glass I'd broken out of the door, but the void remained. I told Nate I'd nail some plywood over it if it was mine. He said he'd get right on it.

I said: "Who drives the ghetto box on the bricks?"

He turned, nodded his head in that direction, said, "Come on. I'll let you ask him."

"Family?"

He hesitated. Then: "That's what I hear."

"Talk to me, Nate."

"Man, I ain't nothing but hired help. Don't get me fired."

I didn't get him fired while he escorted me through the house to the lanai again.

Nate drifted deftly and I stepped down the short stair.

Iveta's irresistible eyes found mine. A smile twisted her mouth and she looked at Sideburns. He sat across the patio table from her and couldn't see me but her reaction informed him someone was behind him.

He turned, saw me. Not much reaction. He said, "I hear you shot my young friend."

"Not me, but if he's old enough to point guns at people, he's old enough to get popped. The fuck are you?"

"His grandfather is not someone you want angry at you."

"I'll be more careful next time he fucks up. I asked who the fuck are you?"

"He's my brother, Duncan. Boris, this is Duncan Sloan, Renaldo's friend you have heard much about."

Boris retrieved a smoke from the ashtray, stuck it in his mouth, rose, hand out like he gave a big shit.

I watched the hand for a couple of beats, letting him know I wasn't gonna be a close friend no matter I was fucking his sister.

I took his paw briefly and we sat.

The whole boy-juice scene amused hell outta Iveta.

Wish I'd been amused. I wasn't but I smiled anyway. If the sincerity police knew how badly I wanted to punch Iveta's scum-ass brother in the fucking Adam's apple, they'd have sent a swat team after me.

Be nice, Sloan. Ask some pertinent questions, watch Boris lie. "You friends with Gene?"

"Eugene? No." Then a cold condescending stare.

"I need more." The air between us is getting thick. I'm thinking only the second coming of Hey-zeus is gonna keep me off this dick.

"I'm not sure that is any of your business. And even if it was, I don't discuss men's business in front of women."

I broke the stare to look at Iveta. She didn't think it was all that funny anymore. She said: "Should I leave?"

I said, "Please." And I'll stick my foot up your brother's ass, wear him around like a bedroom slipper for a few days.

Brother Boris said, "Relax, Mr. Sloan. I was only putting you on a little. My sister tells me that my brother-in-law has retained an old friend to look into his, ah, troubles. I wanted to see if you were up to the task. Surely you can understand, considering my brother-in-law." A little wink came with it, no charge.

"Considering what?"

He shrugged like he didn't give much of a shit one way or another. "He is rather, ah, bookish, wouldn't you say?"

I killed the piece of fuck with my eyes. Driving Rennie's car, so I'm pretty damned sure he's living off Rennie's money. Fucking around in Rennie's business on the sly. A total gypsy piece of shit and he sits over there calling Rennie a nance. I knew Ren was a nance. Hell, Ren knew he was a nance. No use making a big deal out of it—it wouldn't increase Boris's manliness a bit.

I looked at Iveta, said, "Now I'm wondering what you must have told him about me." To the brother: "Tell me where you fit. Make it brief and make it as factual as you're able to."

Boris showed me how cool and collected he was, fired up another butt with the previous one still smoldering in the ashtray, poured himself coffee from a carafe, added dark liqueur from a cut decanter. "I know about the girl."

I took it well if it was supposed to shock me. "How? Firsthand?" And I smiled.

Made Boris smile back. "No, Mr. Sloan, I didn't kill her. Renaldo himself told me. I was, ah, a policeman in Minsk. I thought maybe I could help." His hands came up in despair. "But here my language and cultural skills are inadequate for such delicate work."

I wondered how his shakedown skills were doing on this side of the pond. "You the one set Rennie up with all these youngbloods walking around with automatic weapons?"

He gave me one of his give-a-shit shrugs. "I am in the security business—your friend seemed to need security."

"He does now. So what's up with you and Eugene?"

He shrugged Gene off. "I talked to him, told him to let me know if anything happened. You and your man show up, rough Eugene up, he comes to see me."

Well, there you go then.

Let's try being real: "I think there's more to it than that. Why's Pat scared of you?"

I watched Iveta. She watched her empty coffee cup. I wondered what her face was doing.

Boris showed me his surprised face. "*Me*? This Pat woman, she is scared of *me*?" Then his innocent face. "I talked to her two times. I barely know the woman. How can I scare her if I barely know her?"

"Beats me, Boris. Could be because you shot Janie Wall in the forehead a couple of times."

"I assure you, I've killed no one."

"Well, I feel better about that. Listen, I'm losing my focus here, so let's make this a wrap. If you had anything to do with that girl's demise, I'll crucify you. I don't give a shit whose brother you are or if you were the Lord High Chancellor of Minsk, I'll fucking fix you."

And I had the bitch, had him in my sights. The cunning motherfucker'd gotten me wondering if my instincts were fritzing a bit. Good slick acting job. But I pushed him just far enough, just quick enough to move him off his blocking. He showed me a flash of a face that had killed a few men, then he hid it just as quickly.

I wondered if he realized he'd slipped. Knowing if he knew would help me later when we crashed into one another.

[20]

Boris left.

Iveta wanted to roll on Rennie's mattress some, but I got my arms around my dignity and my ethics, said I had to go.

She pouted a bit and, as pouts go, it wasn't a bad one. I stood unaffected and left with some words in her native tongue I'm glad I didn't understand.

Rolled along, the Vette being as docile and steady as Sancho Panza's donkey. I needed the tranquility the semi-autopilot offered my taxed brain. Last report, it had been spotted around Alpha Centauri and moving fast outbound.

I flowed across the earthly plain; I floated in a nothing-filled void.

I should walk away.

I could walk away—fuck Rennie, the lying fuck. And I really didn't owe anybody else shit. Didn't owe Janie Wall's progeny shit. And double fuck Booker.

Okay: I'm walking. Felt better immediately. Blew out some breath, expressing the problem at the windshield like a voodoo priest. Better still.

Sure it was better. I was whistling in the dark and I knew it. I'd never gotten off that easy in my fucking life. Even my cell knew the score so it chirped and vibrated where it lay on the console, just in case I'd forgotten.

So sorry, off work until further notice.

The little piece of electronics shuddered at me, letting me know I had an urgent and important message in queue.

Fuck it. I said I was done with this charade.

A minute or so the piece shuddered again.

I peek. Not a familiar set of numerals on caller ID.

I watched a curious finger push a button. A mechanical voice told me I had an unheard message, then: "Mr. Sloan, I'm sorry to bother you. This is Lavonne Wall. I got your number from Officer Booker. I hope it's alright I called." We took a pause, collected our thoughts, then, "If you could possibly call us and let us know if you've heard anything. Uh, I know we just saw you this morning, but..." Another pause. It was hard for her to ask things of a near-stranger. "But these boys have been a mess since we went and saw Officer Booker. Felix can't stop crying and Trevor's in his room and won't speak to anybody." More Pause. "I guess what I'd like is just a phone call even if you haven't heard anything. Thank you and good bye. Oh, here's our phone number..." Got digits.

Goddam motherfucking son of a goddam bitch.

I slid the sunroof back, held up a big, sincere fuck-you finger at God. You're a busy little fucker, aren't you? Got nothing else to do but lay about all day eating locusts and honey and fucking with me.

I grinned, told the sunroof, "Fat fucking chance, dad. This time *you* lose— I'm done here."

Closed the roof, ground my eyeteeth against each other until my jaw hurt.

When I got through with damning God and daring him to show his inconstant face, I damned Booker for a while. Then I did what I knew I'd do all along—scrolled to Lavonne Wall's number and punched redial.

Mrs. Wall helloed me; I identified myself and apologized. "I really don't have much to tell you, ma'am. I'm talking to people and trying to figure it all out. I'm sorry."

"Well, like I said in my message, it's only been a few hours since we saw you, but these boys need to hear something from somebody besides me."

I could hear a television babbling its nonsense in the background.

"Could I talk to Trevor?"

"I'll see. Hold on."

Off-line: "Felix, its Mr. Sloan. You want to talk to him?" Felix says, *yeah.*

"Hold on, Mr. Sloan. Here's Felix. I'll go get Trevor."

I held on—timorously.

"Mr. Sloan?" A small voice, stuffed-nosed.

"Hey, Felix. How's it going?"

"Not too good. You find out who killed our mom?"

"I'm getting close, Felix." I hoped I was. "I've been investigating all day." I searched for a grain of positiveness, found little, offered: "I'll find whoever did it. I promise you that, buddy."

"Okay. Will you call us when you find out?"

"Absolutely. Be patient for me, okay?"

"Okay. Here's Gramma."

"Bye, kiddo."

He said his goodbye, handed me to Gramma.

"I'm sorry, Mr. Sloan, but I can't get Trevor to open his door. He's been in there all day, hasn't eaten a thing, won't answer me. Should I try to break the door?"

Jesus, lady, you're asking *me* for child-rearing advice?

Fuck.

"Where do you live?"

She told me. Was way the hell and back south of town, a respectable lower-middle cut.

"You mind if I drop by, talk to Trevor?"

"Oh, would you? Please, would you? He's got no one, no men anyway. No father, no uncles, no one. Would you be so kind?"

No, I wouldn't be so kind, but I've got this tumor on my conscience, see...

***

The little house was straight from the book of subdivision houses. Squat. Minimal 3/12 roof with defeated single-tabs doing their best to keep out the sky and its tricks. Minimal stucco over cinder block so crazed and chipped it looked like an impossible puzzle with a few pieces missing. A dappled compact sat quietly under a flat-roofed carport. One of the carport's posts had been bumped over six or eight inches and the roof swooped down capriciously over it. But the paint was so-so fresh and the yard was neat and trimmed. A hedge older than my car skulked near the house with a soldier missing from the ranks here and there.

The curb was one of those rolling jobs they apply to the neighborhoods that can't afford to complain. I surfed over it, hobbled my ride on the parkway in accordance with local fashion.

The driveway strips went straight while a narrow walk veered toward the low porch. There were a couple of wrought-iron bouncers, a few flowing potted plants and a door with three little stair-stepped windows in it. The glass in the door had been denied its life-purpose by a layer of foil.

I could hear a television on the other side of the door. I put quiet knucks to the rippled veneer.

I got a, “Come in,” from the inside.

I tried the knob. It complied and I went in.

Mrs. Wall was on a soft plaid couch. Felix was out, head in her lap. She laid a gentle palm over his exposed ear, used a remote to drop the TV noise. “Hi, Mr. Sloan. Thanks for coming.”

I spoke as softly as my bass-clef frog's croak allows, said, “Don't mention it. How's the little man?” and nodded at Felix.

She smiled, her eyes inadvertently darted to the idiot box then to me. “He's better. After he talked to you, he quit crying and ate a decent dinner. Thank you.”

I nodded. “Trevor still holed up in his cave?”

“Yes. I hear his music, so I know he's in there, but that's all I get.” She glanced at the tube, pointed with the remote, chased the audio away. “Please, sit down.”

I picked a bent-wood rocker with a cross-stitched cushion tied to it. The cushion invited me to sit down, take a load off. I accepted, sat.

"Mrs. Wall, please understand, this business goes slowly. Bad guys don't walk up, admit their sin. That's why it's called investigation."

"I understand you're not the police, Mr. Sloan."

"No. I don't have access to the things Lieutenant Booker does. I have a computer but we don't get along." Hell, I couldn't even stop that annoying persistent McAfee box from popping up every time I used the machine, and I didn't know why those Adobe people kept bothering me to update—the only reference I had to adobe surely wasn't computer related. Last adobe I saw was looking out the window of a federal prison at the Indian reservation next door. But.... "But, because I'm not, I do enjoy certain luxuries the authorities aren't allowed." Like sticking mokes in the freezer, washing their hair in a public toilet. "But, again, all I've got is a gun, a car, a bag of tricks and a powerful jawbone I use for lying, threatening and fending off right-hooks. I run a primitive game, ma'am, but I end up with pretty decent results. If I give my word I'll do something, I'll do it, whatever it takes. I gave my word to these boys I'd find who did this and I'd fix them. And that's what I'll do."

The eyes took advantage of my running out of breath, glanced at the TV. "What's *fix*, Mr. Sloan?"

I shrugged. I'd rather she hadn't asked. "Send them to jail if I can. That takes rock-solid evidence." Another shrug, this issue more apologetic. "I don't always get it."

She killed the tube, put the eyes on me undistractedly. "What if that happens?"

"We just have to play it out, see how it falls."

She knew a dodge when she heard one. She said, "You're scaring me some, Mr. Sloan."

"Yes, ma'am." I scare me sometimes. "Can I give it a go with Trevor?"

Mrs. Wall watched me a while more. I suspected she was wondering if she wanted someone like me associating with her grandkids.

"Down the hall. At the end. You'll hear the music." More earnest stare. Then: "Mr. Sloan, these children can't take anymore. If something crazy happens, please don't let us know."

"Granted." I rose, crossed the braided rug, stepped off onto the ambered terrazzo. The television crackled behind me. The volume went up on canned laughter. I suspected the only laughing around here for a while had been of that canned variety.

My ears led me down a dark hallway to a door that began life as a simple lauan slab. Now it was flat black. Face-level, a drawing of a menacing white skull with fluorescent yellow teeth glared at me with bold-red eyes. Under the skull the word *peligro* was misspelled as *pelagro* in bold-red letters. At first glance I though it was referencing the vitamin deficiency.

Jack White, in one of his never ending incarnations, was making the door bulge and the hinges creak with that old Valco Airline of his. I'd heard it before; he was bitching about dying by the drop. I could commiserate.

Knuckled up the lauan, said, "Trevor."

Nada.

Put the heel of my fist to task. Made the door bounce. "Trevor, it's Sloan."

The music went low.

"Open up, dude, it's Sloan."

Got an invite to go fuck myself.

"Pal, you don't open this goddam door, I'll pick the lock."

Got wished good luck on the bluff and an invite to go to hell.

I caught movement at the edge of my eye. Turned and saw Mrs. Wall watching from the other end of the hall. She saw me look, shrugged, shook her mop. "That's all he did for me: curse at me."

Yeah, but only because you tolerate it, ma'am. "Let me handle this. Go back and enjoy your show." She nodded and disappeared.

I turned back to Trevor's door, told it: "Last chance, Trev. Open it."

"Fuck you."

I twisted the knob. It rolled in my hand but I got stymied by a hasp and a padlock on the inside.

Check my rearview. No Mrs. Wall so I gently shouldered the danger door open. It gave with a creak and opened, the entire six-foot-plus piece of casing going with it. The casing swung spastically then dangled from the hasp like a hanged man. The music died.

Trevor said, "You fucked up my door."

I stepped in, pushed the door and its captive casing shut with my ass.

We watched each other a while then Trevor repeated the complaint verbatim. He stood by a desk, with a boom-box on it.

I crossed the mess that was his room, scrunched down and got as in his face as much as the difference in our weight classes would let me.

He flinched a little, but—bless him—the little fucker held his ground.

I said, from all up in his face, "And you're fucking up your gramma's life. What? You don't think this thing's as hard on her as it is you? That was your mom but it was her child, part a her just like you're part a your mom. You straighten your goddam ass up, act like some-fucking-body here."

Trevor's eyes came off mine, went in the direction of the door. I turned, said, "We're having a man-to-man here, ma'am, if you don't mind."

She nodded a sage gramma nod, said, "No, I don't think I mind at all. Excuse me."

The door made soft complaints and Trevor's gaze came back to me when I turned.

Tried going lateral, looking for common footing.

"I heard The Dead Weather. You into the Raconteurs, too?"

A bony shrug, averted eyes. "Yeah, alright. I like The Dead Weather better."

"Yeah, I'm getting there myself. Took a while, though. You listening to Cage the Elephant?"

A grin, "In one ear..."

I said, "...and out the other. Your granny let you listen to that stuff?"

Another bony shrug, a scrunched face. "She doesn't know. She just sits and looks at her shows mostly." He sat in the desk chair, began fiddling with the boomer.

I looked around. A cheap black-on-white Fender Squire and a pig-nose amp. A wall of girlie posters I wouldn't have let my thirteen, fourteen-year-old exhibit. Another wall was the same black as the door, had big-headed monsters devouring little guys in suits and ties. Drippy letters over it, done in orange, said: *Aliens Eat Corporate Stooges.* It was a pretty good piece in a clean, anime sort of way. Another wall in flat purple and another in the yellow from the skull's teeth bore similar neat drawings with juvenile impeachments of society.

"You paint this stuff?"

"Yeah." Obviously aware of his knack.

"Not bad. You ever take lessons?"

"What? Art lessons?"

"Yeah."

He poo-pooed me. "Nah. I just do it."

"You enjoy a little tagging now and again?"

We grinned at each other conspiratorially.

"Some. My gramma doesn't like that much. She's afraid I'll get arrested by the police."

"They're the guys who'll do it. Look, Trevor, I haven't found out much yet. I've located my friend, the one your mom worked for. I got some good leads from him. I told you and Felix I'd take care of this and I will. I promise you."

He wasn't sold in spite of my musical prowess. "I don't believe in promises anymore."

Oh my.

"I know this is hard on you and Felix."

"Yeah? How would you know? Your mom ever been killed?"

Not a good time, but I laughed a little.

Trevor asked, "Why's that funny?"

"Because I do know, dude. You're thirteen, I was seventeen. You got me there, but, yeah, Trev, I know how it feels."

We watched the other. We both wanted him to believe me.

Finally: "Who was it killed your mom?"

"Believe it or not, Trevor, was pirates. Not the Johnny Depp kind—real pirates of the Caribbe."

"Yeah. I've seen 'em on cable news. Little black dudes. Got speedboats."

"Close enough. Was a pirate name of Pomme de Terre. Know what that means in French?"

"Un-un."

"The Potato." I grinned.

He laughed a low boy-man giggle. "Mr. Potato Head."

I said, "Who's laughing now?"

"You serious?"

"Sadly, yeah. My dad too. The guy your mom worked for? His parents were with them."

His fingers fidgeted with a seam on his corduroy skinnies. "You ever find this Potato guy?"

"No." Not yet, Trevor. But I'm still breathing, so don't count me down. No way I could say what I was thinking. I went into this thing in hopes of keeping these boys from growing up trying to find their own Pomme de Terre.

"He'd be old now, wouldn't he?"

Smart kid. "Yeah, I guess. I try not to dwell on it much." Big fat one there: I thought about it quite often. I didn't care how old the fucker got. If I found him, I'd assume him still guilty.

"I try, but I can't stop thinking about my mom. I..." He turned away abruptly, pressed a hand over his mouth.

"Trevor, I know how it feels when that bond just disappears." I regrouped, simplified. "There's this thing that lives between a mother and a son, and when it goes away or gets broken, it hurts, dude, I won't kid you. It hurts a long time and it hurts bad. But it will get better with time. The anger and helplessness'll slowly turn into the good memories you keep of your mom. Hang on, little brother, it'll get bearable."

He turned and we watched each other through prisms of tears.

I said, "You want us to sit here and have a crying jag or you want us to man up, go get a couple, three third-pounder Beefy King Deluxes?"

Trevor opted for the beef.

***

We pumped our egos back up to manly-status with lots of good USDA inspected grade-A American beef. Would be no more tears from us carnivores tonight.

We rode a bit, digesting, Trevor fiddling with my stereo. We were rocking Beggars' Banquet and I was shocked he was digging it. Parachute Woman came up and I thought he was going to beat my dashboard to death. This kid's stock was going up on my little Wall Street.

Loose cash, a Gandhi store and a gush of generosity collided a few blocks from the Wall house. We went in and I covered my new little buddy on the cheesy cell phone of his choice, told the clerk to do us gobs of minutes and all the bells and whistles available.

"Trev, tell the man what you want."

Trevor went un-speechless, said, "Everything."

I said, "Wise choice." To the happy amber clerk: "Could you put that in a bag to go?"

He said he'd put it in anything I wanted.

Trevor and I exited the store and one of us was so deep into the grid I had to quick-step to keep that one from creaming his new global-connector into the glass doors.

Rolling again, Trevor surprised me: he put the phone in his lap, said, "Can I ask you somethin?" Serious now.

I wasn't sure but said, "Shoot."

Fiddle with the phone, then: "Why're you being so nice to us?"

"Why shouldn't I be?"

Bony-shouldered shrug. "I don't know. I mean, you're not a policeman. People gotta pay you, don't they? I mean, cops are nice to people cause that's their job."

First I'd heard about that. "Don't worry about it."

Some quiet. Some: "How much do you charge?"

I laughed a little inside. "Depends."

Some more quiet, then: "How much would you charge for something like our mom getting killed?"

"Don't worry about it. I've got you covered."

Thought I'd placated his curiosity since he lifted the phone, pushed it in the face some. I eaves-dropped but he was a quiet phoner.

"Hey, Gramma, it's me. Is Felix there?"

Pause.

"Mine."

Pause.

"Mr. Sloan wanted to be able to get me anytime." He looked at me, grinned at the near-lie.

"No, I didn't spend my money. Could I talk to Felix—please?"

Pause, a *hey* into the phone, then he turned away and mumbled at his brother.

The mumbling got serious then got aggressive, then quiet again. Trevor killed the phone, glanced at me then away.

We rode in silence the couple of blocks to his house and I wasn't sure if he was pissed or what. Quiet kids are hard studies.

I rolled across the low curb, shut the Vette down, said, "You cool?"

I surprised him back from deep thought. "Yeah," like why wouldn't he be. "Can you wait a minute? Felix is bringing something."

"Sure."

And Felix was hanging in Trevor's window with a quart Mason jar. He jingled it, handed it to Trevor.

Trevor took the jar, said, "Okay, thanks. Go back inside."

Felix leaned out of the window, said, "It's my money too."

"Beat it, aquarium breath."

Me: "Hey."

Trevor: "Sorry."

Felix: "Can I stay, Mr. Sloan?"

My mouth was going to agree but Trevor chopped me off. "No. Me and Mr. Sloan got business to discuss. Beat it."

I looked at Felix, shrugged. He went into a pout, turned to go.

Trevor pulled a bag of burgers from the back, said, "Here, brat, I brought you some Beefy Kings."

Felix didn't turn back, just yelled how he didn't want any stupid Beefy Kings.

When he'd closed the door harder than Gramma woulda liked, Trevor said, "Me and Felix combined our money and got a hundred and seven dollars and fifty-six cents." An odd pause. "Is that enough?"

Ah man. Ah Jesus. Ah God. Ah shit.

Lately, seems I'm asking myself *why me?* more than Alfred E. fucking Neuman.

Left Trevor with a better outlook, the bag of burgers for Gramma and his brother, and my cell number with instructions to call me anytime—no, *anytime*—at all. And of course, his glorious new handful of silicon chips with about a gazillion cell minutes.

I turned around, pointed myself in the direction of what I call home with a hefty seven-dollars-and-fifty-six-cent retainer in my pocket.

I didn't know how I felt right then.

[21]

All but crib-wise, Raleigh cells, asks do I wanna see what Gene looks like dead.

"Ah, man."

"Un-huh. Lemme complicate for you. They's two more dead in one of them addresses you gave me. Another one looks like somebody's been slaughtering pigs in there. The other three, ain't nobody around and don't look like anybody's been around."

"Sounds like somebody just stomped on Rennie's commercial arm. How about the Pat girl?"

"I went by, told her to get her shit and get gone."

"What'd she say?"

"She was already packing. Asked would I mind watching out while she got the fuck outta there."

"Good. I met Sideburns."

"Yeah?"

"Yeah. We need a sit-down."

"Sound like it. Who's the man?"

"Brother Boris. He's just helping out's how I heard it."

"Mmm. Funny didn't nobody mention no Boris."

"Yeah, ain't it funny? I'll be doing lunch at Johnson's Diner, noon tomorrow," and dropped him before he could rally on an alternative.

Only way Raleigh could hurt my billfold at Miz Johnson's was if he ate the whole place: bricks, mortar, parking lot and flatware.

I hit Rennie one-handed, caught a downtown exit.

Of course he didn't answer. The mad professor has no time for murder or mayhem. He's got a Sloan for that.

Message: *Ren, your houses are shut down. Call.* Killed the connection.

Two minutes, Ren hits me back. I go: "Why the fuck didn't you mention your asshole brother-in-law?"

"Why should I?"

"He knew about Janie Wall."

"So?"

"You didn't ask him to apply his Eastern-Bloc police expertise to the situation?"

"Hell no. Iveta asked if I wanted him to help and I told her I'd rather call you. You called me first though, didn't you?"

Yes I did. "Then why's he mucking around in your business, scaring people?"

"First I've heard about it. Want me to speak to him?"

I didn't buy that shit for a second. "No need now. Rennie, someone's killing your people, running the rest off. You're effectively out of business."

"No big."

I exercised my right to an extended pause. Then I go: "'Scuse me? What's *no big*, Ren? Dead employees, being outta business? What?"

"None of it. Medical genetics, Sloan, that's the new frontier. Even the legit medical community's recognized the general-analgesic benefits of cannabis for centuries and today's technology is pushing it into turbo mode. Bro, I'm seriously about three backcrosses from a fucking cure for the migraine headache—a fucking cure. Besides that, I'm producing a full retail line of nutrients, additives, soil mixes—my own gear label. Designer beans that'll flip whatever recreational wig you feel like wearing. I'm taking the show to Canada, pal, going semi-legal. Fuck the grow biz. It was nothing more than a means to an end. Now, I've got the ends. I'm gonna *own* this fucking industry."

"Rennie, stop and think now, bro." I'm talking nice and slow, being a *bro*. "Think about how what you're saying sounds. What about Janie Wall? What about a couple more dead at another house? Come on, Ren."

"*Come on*? You come on. They knew the risks. They knew what they were doing was illegal. Shit happens."

"They were growing pot, Rennie. They weren't selling AK's to Mariolettos or cooking meth at the Econolodge."

"Sloan, I gotta go. Got a conference call with British Columbia coming in. Clean this mess up, okay? I got fifty grand with your name on it. Ciao, baby."

I had to fucking pull over when he hung up I was so fucking bothered. *Ciao? Designer beans?*

But the most bothersome part of all? How the hell does a guy with an obvious passion to cure people of migraines and such have absolutely no compassion whatsoever for people getting their frontal lobes blown through the backs of their heads? Maybe it was just Ren's fucked up brain had decided to take the stroll down the old socio path.

Oh my, oh my. My list of asses I'd like to kick just kept growing. I puffed air at the windshield and drove on to the crib with surprising serenity and an empathy for my fellow travelers I seldom exhibit.

Opened my door to the landline demanding attention. Took my time getting a light on; the phone went mum. Then started up again with its demands.

Check caller ID: the Bellagio. Oh, now who could that be at this fine hour?

Lemme guess: "Whassup, Paulie?"

"Sloan, Sloan, Sloan. The fuck do you keep getting into these situations?"

"I don't know, Paulie. I try to live right, be charitable, tolerant of my fellow man and it still happens."

"Yeah, me too. I called Booker earlier today. He says you got 'em dropping like flies around you."

"I don't know that *I've* got 'em dropping. But, yeah, lots a dropping going on. What else did Booker have to say?"

"Not much. Said something about accessory to everything from murder to illegal dumping."

"Accessory to who?"

"I think that's: *to whom.*" Pause. "He doesn't know?"

"Un-un."

"Do you?"

"Un-huh. Wanna hear about it?"

He wanted to hear. I told it, no holds barred.

The part about Dennis and the freezer, he stopped me. "Whoa. Back up a verse, Sloan. You and Raleigh put a state parole officer in a freezer?"

"Yeah. It wasn't frost-free either and I feel bad about that."

Paulie huffed. "Shit, Sloan. What's his name? I'll see what I can do."

"You can't do shit for him, Paulie. Let's just say he's not a problem anymore."

"He one of the flies Booker mentioned dropping?"

"Yeah."

"You drop him?"

"Nope, not me."

"Raleigh?"

"Un-un."

"You know who did?"

"Don't have to worry about them either."

"Them? Holy Jesus. I can't believe Booker's letting you walk the streets."

"Me either. Wanna hear some more?"

"No, but go ahead."

I went ahead. Got past Dennis and the rest area situation, fucking Iveta, my visit with Booker and the Wall family.

Paulie caught a space, wanted to hear more about me fucking Iveta. I told him let's keep it professional. He touché-ed with: "Like you while you were fucking your client's wife?" I told him to dick his short self and finished up the confession with meeting Boris at Rennie's.

"And that's it, Paulie."

"Oh? That's all?" Long breathy *fuck.* Then, "I'll be in Sunday about three. You need to pick me up and see if we can keep the sentencing part of your trial at least tolerable."

"You think you can keep me outta jail?"

"Anybody see you shoot anybody?"

"Un-un." Not yet.

"Then we're cool. Call you when I'm on the tarmac." Pause. "And please try to keep it to a dull roar till I hit the ground."

"I'll try, Paulie. How's Vegas?"

"Ah, Sloan. There was this private show out at one of the raunch ranches had an orangutan, big fucking wooly bastard, hung like a..."

I killed the call. I'd heard it from Paulie before. Different species, same story with the same happy ending.

[22]

Applied somniferents to my brain again, slept like crap for it again. Narcotics are fantastic for the free of conscience, I suppose. The rest of us sleep like death for three, four hours then flop for a few more. Then wake early feeling like shit.

Poured tons of coffee on my brains-of-peanut-butter, fussed and fretted with the morning. I couldn't sit still. I paced. When the coffee kicked in and defrosted my windshield I still couldn't see shit.

Something. Something was going on. It involved me and I was the only one involved who didn't have a clue.

Needed food. My cupboard was near bare. I chopped up a hotdog, browned it a bit, scrambled two eggs over it, ate it on a long-lost hamburger bun I found skulking in the freezer compartment.

The grub relaxed me and I let the troubles go. I dozed on the couch until it was almost time to meet Raleigh, woke refreshed and hungry—a wonderful condition to be in for a visit to Miz Johnson's diner.

Called Raleigh. I'd intended to remind him about lunch but ended up annoying him. Enough so he had to remind me he had devices that told him when he needed to shit, and he didn't need me wasting his cell minutes. So I hung up, skied out for downtown.

***

Raleigh and I did a decent synchronized arrival, bumped knucks and went in the little cinder-block box that was Johnson's Diner. I hadn't been in for a while so Miz Johnson asked Raleigh who his friend was, teasing me. Raleigh said we weren't friends. Me and Miz Johnson laughed about it.

Excellent soul food got washed down with too-sweet iced tea. Raleigh and I quietly damaged ourselves as we often do at Miz Johnson's.

I'd had fried chicken so I excused myself and went to wash. The Men's is outside, around a corner. Parked near its door was a tall pick-up that reminded me of things.

Washed up, dried my hands on my pants and dialed Booker. It rang and I walked, went back in and sat—still ringing.

Message: Blah-blah, leave a number.

I left: "Booker, call me. I wanna know who owned the pick-up that was cutting up at Dennis Toussaint's going-away party at the rest area. It should be on the surveillance video." Folded the phone.

Raleigh degreased with a beat-up napkin. Said, "Why didn't you ask about the SUV and the Cadillac?"

"No way they were running straight plates on those bad boys. They planned on tossing hull from those vehicles. The four-wheeler's a maybe. Since it was in and out so quick, maybe they didn't worry about it."

"That don't click, then what else you got?"

I sat, thought. Said: "Nothing. I got nothing else."

My phone chirped. Booker.

I go: "Hey."

"Mr. Sloan. I was just cogitating on callin you and you call me."

"Yeah? What were you calling about?"

"This is good: bout what you called *me* about is what I was callin *you* about."

"Great minds, what can I say? What's the deal on our truck?"

"Was stole." Enough quiet to say he wanted me to play.

"Yeah? From who?"

A chuckle. "You know, you always surprise me, Sloan. I go to thinkin how you a dumb, lazy no-good, and you come up with somethin damn near brilliant. Sure do."

"Why's it good and why're you laughing?"

"It's two different things. It's good cause a who owns the stole truck. I'm laughin cause after you came in yesterday with all this news about that rest area shoot out, I got to wonderin just how deep you—and prob'ly Raleigh—was in this thing. So what I did, see, was grab me one a them techies downstairs, got him to bring up one a his big screens. So when he got here we went back and looked at the video. That's when we seen the Lincoln."

The fucker let the beat drop, sat on it because I wasn't touching it.

Booker said, "I said we seen the Lincoln on the videos. You hear me?"

Raleigh was picking his teeth with a pinky nail so I looked at him and said, "What Lincoln?"

Booker laughed, said, "Come on, Sloan. I got ya'll all over that fuckin Lincoln. No plates but how many eighty-six Town Cars still rollin? Guy Raleigh bought it offa described him right down to the limp and the bad attitude."

"How's that affecting me?" I was guessing the videos weren't high-def enough for him to make me and Raleigh.

More laugh, and he sounded genuinely amused. "Get this. They dust this Lincoln—oh yeah, we found ya'll's dead boys in the trunk—guess who's prints is on one a the fenders. Go on, Sloan, Guess."

I guessed Puggy Feinstein but was wrong.

"My lil ole intern sends this print off to Washington, national data base. Gotta hit too. Federal felon name a Duncan Sloan. Know 'im, Sloan?"

"Come on, Booker."

"*Come on*? *Come on*? Sloan, I got five dead folks—no, six countin Wackenhut. You fuckin come on. How many *is* dead?

How many I don't know about yet? We gone need to build a new wing on the fuckin morgue fore you get done helpin your friend?"

"Hang on, Booker, I'll see?" I put the phone away from my ear, asked Raleigh, "How many dead did you find?"

Raleigh played along. "Two at the one house, Gene at his house, but whoever was in the other place either is dead or in the hospital."

I put the phone back to my face, said, "Only three more confirmed." Did it tight mouthed.

"*Only three more* makes nine. You and Raleigh didn't feel no obligation to mention bout dead folks out on the Four?"

"I told you about the rent-cop when I saw you. You already knew about the girl in the trunk and the parole guy. Now you found some guys in some Lincoln. So what you want, Booker? Want me to get out there amongst 'em, start throwing just so I'll have something to tell you? Goddam, get off my fucking back."

Raleigh looked up at me; I grinned through gritted teeth. He looked disappointed in me, went back to his pecan pie.

"Gimme them addresses where ya'll found them dead people. And why the fuck didn't you mention your friend Alvarez being Mister-Fucking-Green-Jeans? Goddam, Sloan."

"I figured you were smart enough to figure it out. Let me tell you something, Booker, all I did was take a call from an old friend in the middle of the fucking night. So you gotta treat me like it's *me* shooting these motherfuckers? I got a couple a kids for clients that *you* set me up with, goddammit. Whatchu want, Lieutenant? Want me to go get shot for free just to make your life easier, ease your conscience?"

"No, Sloan, that's exactly what I don't want. Word on the street is your buddy's in a full-fledge turf war over his many sins. I'm tryin to tell you don't fuck around and get yourself shot over some goddam dope-dealin mess, you dumb-ass."

We took a long pause, chilled it back a touch.

Booker eased up, said, "You think you can keep it under an even dozen?"

"I can try, Booker."

We took another good pause.

"Sloan, I may a made a mistake throwin that old woman and them young'uns in your face like that. Listen to me when I tell you don't fuck around and let that messed up sense of justice get you in dutch nowhere. You hear me?"

"I hear. You gonna let me and Raleigh run with this?"

"Who I got work here as results oriented as you and Raleigh?"

[23]

Raleigh wanted to know why Nookie Hazboun would own a mudbogger.

"Don't know, Raleigh. Maybe he went to trade school, learned a vocation requires a truck."

Not likely though. I was thinking it; Raleigh said it, said: *Please. Nookie ain't messing with nothing that's the slightest bit legal.*

Nookie was an F1 issue of Palestinian immigrants, their youngest. Pop was an upstanding citizen—if naturalized—and a monied asset to his community and his mosque. Nookie wasn't.

Nookie'd been tossed out and welcomed back so many times he probably had a T-shirt said *Prodigal Son* on it. I knew—I'd played a bit part, fetched Nook home a time or two for Pops, paid off some tough boys a few times who'd get Nookie hiding from his shadow. The usual rich-boy sins: drugs, gambling, whores.

But now Nook was all grown up, late twenties somewhere. Word was, Pops had all but weaned Nookie off the honey tit. Nookie went entrepreneurial in response, was a wanna-be-gangster now. Had himself a crew of short, dark fucks with plenty of hardware, had a frighteningly quiet Indian-American kid name of Shaq playing Meyer Lansky for him. Nookie's not much in the attic but insulation—he needs a Lansky to count past ten for him.

I tossed a couple of twenties on the twelve dollar check, said: "Wanna go ask?"

"Booker give you his address?"

"Yeah, but he won't be home; he never is. I used to babysit him, remember. I know where Fadi Korbani'll be."

"Un-huh. That road'll lead to Rome, won't it? Where's the Fad-man hawking Slurpee these days?"

My data on Fadi was from his being a childhood friend and reliable conspirator of Nookie's.

Raleigh had experienced Fadi himself a couple years back. Fadi'd sucker punched Raleigh in the face that episode and Raleigh—hearsay, didn't personally witness—shredded the pudgy motherfucker. At the jail, Fadi gets out after a toss, blames Raleigh for holding up his paperwork. Raleigh admits it, tells Fadi to get the fuck off county property while he's still got two legs. Fadi blind-side hooks Raleigh as he walks by. As has been said: Raleigh shredded the fucker while nobody saw nothing.

"Same old. State Store, downtown."

"He got a liquor license, didn't he?"

"Un-huh."

"Damn, Sloan, how's a motherfucker like Fadi Korbani get a liquor license?"

"Four hundred large. The brokers don't care who the fuck you are much. I don't know as Fadi's ever done a felony. Mostly locked up for having too much fun, wasn't it? You'd know better'n me on Fadi."

Raleigh nodded. "Mostly was just showing out. A gun thing his daddy bought down to a lesser." A shrug like: *who cares?*

Who did care? I didn't. Not anymore, not much.

***

Back in Raleigh's Acura; my sled cooling heel at Miz Johnson's. *Five-Minute Parking*, Orange Av, downtown. Raleigh nabs an empty parallel slot.

"Five minutes gonna do it?"

Raleigh looked over, wagged his head. "Who needs five minutes? If Fadi's here I'll be right back with him." He waited on a break in on-coming, made his break for Fadi's slushee and hootch emporium.

Maybe a minute? I see Raleigh come from the store, little round Fadi at his heels. Man, I love working with psychos—it's entertaining as well as painfully efficient and effective.

Doors opened and a Raleigh and a Fadi got in.

Fadi went familiar, said, "Hey, Sloan. How's it hangin?" Throwing cool, talking gangster.

"Fadi, you gonna give Raleigh the pleasure of kicking your ass?"

Fadi laughed back there in the backseat.

"Not kidding, Fadi."

"Whatchu want, Sloan? Come on. Let's be chill, huh?"

"Sure. You know what I want? Nookie, baby, I want a big ol' piece a Nookie."

Quiet.

"Come on, Fadi, he wasn't one of the boys in the trunk of the Lincoln."

Fadi let some air go through slack lips back there. "Oh, Jesus, Sloan." Beat. "Crazy shit, huh?"

"You tell me, Fadi."

"Un-un. Nook can tell it, he wants to. I ain't talkin shit about these people he's fuckin with. Raleigh, you can kick my ass, I ain't talkin about 'em."

Raleigh hit a red, looked back at Fadi. He could have been amused. He said, "Put us in front a Nookie, Fadi. Like right now."

"I'll call him."

Raleigh said, "You try, I'll stop and break all your stubby little fingers. Which way?"

Fadi said "Straight on like you goin, blood."

Raleigh told him he wasn't his blood. Told Fadi if he tried to jump out and run he wouldn't make it.

Fadi told Raleigh he wouldn't dream of such antics. Said Nookie wasn't his dog anymore. Said Nookie was fucking him over just like everybody else now. Said Nook did his crooked business outta his girlfriend's perfume shop.

Raleigh and I traded looks. The light fell green and Raleigh rolled on.

I said, "You see this coming together, don't you?"

Raleigh said, "Un-huh. Could be a different perfume shop."

"Yeah. Could be. Got a hundred you wanna lose betting it is?"

Fadi was still back there blabbing on with details of how Nook had fucked him.

[24]

We were familiar with the lay so Raleigh dropped it around back. No Escalades back there. Fadi pointed out a door when Raleigh asked which one. Raleigh parked dead in front of the metal door.

I walked Fadi to the traffic door, made him do the secret knock and poor Nookie got punched dead in the face when he opened the door. Fadi punched him, not me. The swat put Nook on his ass.

Then Fadi called Nookie seven or eight sorts of motherfucker in several languages. And here I was—trying not to have any fun.

Nookie got up mouthy so Raleigh stepped in and nailed him in earnest. Sat him back on his ass.

I stepped in the back door and yelled, "Sophia, it's Sloan. Don't call the cops."

Some quiet but for Nookie on his ass grunting, then, "Don't hurt him bad, Sloan, okay?" Was Nookie's girl Sophia but she didn't show herself.

"I'll try not to. You have a good one, sweetie."

Raleigh kicked Nookie, not hard but the drama was enough Fadi ran in, girlie-punched Nookie in the back of the head. The Nook lay back, groaned some for us.

Raleigh grabbed one of Nookie's legs, told Fadi to take the other. They slid him out of the shop and around to the rear of Raleigh's car. All I had to do was lock up behind us.

We loaded up and rode on—*tres amigos* with some junk in the trunk. I looked at Raleigh at the wheel. No look back. I turned and looked at Fadi. He seemed pleasant, sprinkled with a confidence I'd not seen in him before.

Raleigh was wheeling and it was his question so I tossed it at him: *where?*

He said, "Somewhere the motherfucker can't run off."

I asked: "He gonna run?"

"Un-huh." Then he took us on a pastoral tour to a pasture. Acres of pasture, probably two hundred.

Per Raleigh's crystal ball, when he let Nookie out of the trunk Nookie sprinted off. Maybe a hundred feet, maybe two hundred, Nook stops, looks around. Dad, it's still a quarter mile to the nearest highway, woods, fence, what the fuck have you.

Nice piece of bluff work: Raleigh pulls, puts lead in the dirt, sights the piece in Nookie's direction. When Nookie turns he thinks Raleigh's shooting at him.

Nookie looks as innocent as he can, hands up high like a TV cop would want. "Goddam, man, don't fucking shoot me."

Raleigh said, "Then get your fool ass over here."

Nookie did as directed but did it cool—hands out at his side in a *why-me?* thing. Had the Nookie-swagger and the accompanying crooked Nookie-smile going. He says, hard-ass, "Fadi, I'm going to plant your faggot ass."

Raleigh was in control of the show though. "We get done, ya'll do what you want to one another. Right now *we* got business."

Fadi must have forgotten his lines; he pulled a little silver revolver and shot Nookie in the side. Nookie grunted, screamed and went face down.

Then Fadi swings around, pops one off at Raleigh but no good on the aim, throwing early as he was still making his turn.

I was already moving, trying to get the fine Nine outta my dungarees and get behind the car at the same time.

Got to the pistol first, pointed it at Fadi and threw some shit at him.

Raleigh synched; Fadi started leaking all over, went down hard and dead. Nookie lay on the Bahia grass, quiet.

When the sound had gone away, Raleigh said, "Why the fuck did the little bastard shoot at *me*?"

"I believe you kicked his ass once upon a time, didn't you?"

"Don't seem like a reason to shoot a motherfucker though."

I pointed out to Raleigh how he worked at a place that trafficked in people who killed each other over Snickers bars.

"Nookie dead?"

I didn't know but I doubted it. Fadi's piece had been a thirty-two or some such nonsense from the sound of it. I said, "Nook, you awake?"

"Yeah." Pained. "That fuck dead?"

"I'd bet on it. How bad you hit?"

Nookie got up on all fours, moaned, sat back on his heels, moaned. He looked at the bloody hole in his shirt, said, "Shit." He pulled his shirttail up, looked at the nasty purple hole in his side-meat, fainted back into the Bahia. Raleigh and I hid our weapons on our persons, double-teamed Nookie into a sitting position, dragged him over to lean against the car.

I squatted in front of him, slapped his slack face gently and spoke his name. His eyes fluttered, rolled upward.

"Where am I?"

"You're in heaven, Nookie. I'm Saint Peter and that's God Almighty behind me there."

Nookie focused, rolled his eyes down to look at me. "Sloan, you gotta get me to a hospital. I'm dying, bro."

"Yeah, yeah, yeah." I stood. "Hear him, Raleigh. He's dying."

"Yeah? Should we call somebody, nine-one-one or somebody?"

I shrugged. "Man, I don't know. If we hadn't had to shoot Fadi..." then let the beat drop.

"Come on, guys. Please. I ain't saying shit about shit. This ain't funny, now. Sloan, you know my old man. He'll pay you whatever you ask if you get me outta here alive."

"Nook, I got so many hundred dollar bills in my underwear drawer I had to throw my socks away and start on that drawer. Now it's all full up. I make any more money, I'll be walking around half-naked." Gave him a nice pause so he could look at his wound in peace. "Wonder does your daddy know who hired you to play court jester in that pick-up truck the other night?" I nodded cordially. "That'd do it. I knew that, shit, Nooks, I'd carry you outta here on my back."

Then we all watched Nookie, see what his life was worth, see what was he most frightened of.

***

Nookie's redemption dirge wasn't easily sung.

I had to prime him with something like: Nook, you dumb-fuck, you gonna lay there in cow shit and die over a son of a bitch like Boris?

He made some sarcastic noise, wrinkled his face, put out the hand he wasn't using to hold his wounded side, but not so Nookie-cool. "You know, then why you asking?"

"Just need to hear you say it, sweetheart."

"Damn. We good? Can we get me outta here?"

My turn for sarcastic utterings, funny faces. Said: "Raleigh, you hear Nookie say a name?"

"Nah. I ain't hearing shit but whining."

"Goddam. *Boris.* Boris the fucking mobster cop. Please, please kill that motherfucker, Sloan."

"You scared, Nookie?"

"Hell yeah, I'm scared, Sloan. The motherfucker killed those three other guys and they spoke the same language as him. Now the crazy bastard's after me. I been in the perfume shop office for three days, that motherfucker coming in a couple times a day looking for me, getting tough with Sophia. Fuck yes it was Boris hired me. Can we get outta here now?"

I watched him, watched Raleigh, grinned. I tossed a hand at the mayhem, said "You know, this is more our style, blood."

"Quicker too, you don't count travel time."

"We'll work on that. Nook, you ready to go home?"

"Home? Fuck you. Take me to the hospital, dude. Please." Not too tough now.

"Your daddy'd have my feet beat I took you to a public hospital all shot up. You wanna call, ask Pops where we should take you, go ahead, babydoll."

"Your friend took my phone."

I told him Raleigh wasn't my friend, called his old man myself. Figured the old boy would rather hear the truth than his son's voice anyway.

[25]

A large black vehicle rendezvoused with us at—get this—at the rest area opposite the one where Toussaint went to see Jesus.

Then I thought about Nookie's girlfriend's perfumery being next door to Boris's hideout. Seemed like too many coincidences but, come on, the metro isn't that fucking big. And, Nookie was a punk. The punk next door. Wasn't him, it'd been another like him—son of a decent, hard-working mom/dad/both, gone seedy because there was nothing left but to go seedy once video games and pounding pud didn't do it anymore.

No, no coincidences. Was just fucking *happenstance*, whatever the high-English-fuck that means.

Dial Ren.

No Ren.

Message: "Your brother-in-law Boris is nasty."

Dial Booker.

Do the old drop it, redial, go straight to voice mail trick.

Message: "Booker, Nookie's at the doctor's. I didn't do it..." Mumbling beside me. "... and Raleigh *says* he didn't do it..." Pause. "But who knows, huh? Nookie talked pretty for us. Raleigh sends his affections. Bye."

Dial.

No Iveta.

Message: "Sweet Pea, you need to call." I stood on it, not so sure what to say. Balls up: "Your big brother's lost my confidence. You need to make me feel good about *you*."

Raleigh looked over, asked as though he wanted to know what time it was: "You gone keep on fucking her then?"

It wasn't really a question and I didn't have an answer.

We rode along, silent. I was into the labyrinth. Didn't know what Raleigh was skulling but I figured the same: survival. The muddy water was clearing up, but that's when it's most precarious—you're in the mix but can't really see anything or anybody. At that moment, you're running blind.

I said, "You know what we need?"

Raleigh says, "Yeah, a psychic with a water-cooled .50."

I said: "Un-un. Some insight into this Boris motherfucker."

I hit my phone.

Message: "Ren, talk to me. I need some dope on b-in-law. He's up to his neck in this little problem of yours..." I paused, said "...whether you're aware of it or not." I disconnected, drifted off, thinking about my annexed statement. Fuck it. If Ren was in it, he'd have to take his lumps with the rest of the bad guys when the deal went down.

Came back to earth, hid the phone, Raleigh says, "I could see who owns the square foot rental he's playing outta."

I shrugged. "Yeah, but it's gonna be in some corp name, vacant-unit status."

"*Cash* status."

"Sue 'em. Ideas?"

More skulling and freeway.

Raleigh drops her in the break-down lane, dials.

Message: "Hey, call."

Like twenty seconds Raleigh's cell gets antsy.

Raleigh: "Yo."

We listen.

Raleigh: "Belarusian. Boris." Spat the strip mall's name out.

Wait.

Raleigh: "Un-huh. We chill on that Steyr?"

Brief pause.

Raleigh: "Everything's for sale, dog."

We listen.

Raleigh. "Cool. Nah, I ain't fucking with 'im, fool I know is. Peace, cuz."

He looks at me, puts the steel in gear, says, "You fucked, Sloan."

"Remind me why."

"Bro Boris is a life-taker. Did it for the government back home. Word is he's over here to take care of a little state business."

"According to who? Boris the Bullshitter?"

More silent asphalt, a little head wag. Near grin, Raleigh says, "You a fucking mess, Sloan."

"Yeah. I keep saying I'm gonna get me a bumper sticker that says so, too. Tell me about Boris."

"My man I was just chatting at? He's in the big club Boris's club looks up to."

"He's Russian."

"Un-huh. He says they all pretty straight folks." Drama pause. "Except your boy Boris and some a his cohorts. My man thinks they looking for a big score to get themselves set up. He says they're getting scary, bringing a lot of attention to everybody, the Russians included. They ain't happy about it."

We tossed all that around some.

"What was the Russian's offer?" I was sure there would be one.

Raleigh looked away from driving. "He says it's worth fifty if Boris was to fall down hard enough he couldn't get up."

"What's he say the Belarusian's are saying about it?"

"Same. He says we oughta talk to them too."

"I expect I will."

"Why's that?"

"The kid you popped? Boris says his granddaddy's a big deal."

"The old man from the clubhouse?"

"That'd be my guess. Maybe I should man-up, go see him."

"Bout time you did something."

"Goddamn, Raleigh, I shot Fadi."

"Shit, I shot him too."

"I shot him first."

"Well, I shot him more worse."

"Come on, you can only get so dead, dad."

"I guess. Reckon they'll ever find Fadi?"

"Yeah. Few days the buzzards'll draw in a ranch hand or somebody." Fadi didn't care who found him. He'd fucked up and stepped into the twilight, earned a master pass on caring.

"You gone tell Booker?"

I thought about it. "Un un. He'll figure it out if they can ID Fadi's bones. I hope I didn't lie to Booker."

"Bout what?"

"I told him I'd try and keep it under a dozen. It's gonna be close."

"Hmm. How many's Fadi make?"

"Ten."

"You thinking Boris, huh?"

"I don't see any way around it, Raleigh. He's eventually going to insist on it. And it's all crazy. Rennie doesn't even want any of it. It probably coulda been Boris's for the asking."

"But you still gone be under a dozen."

"Yeah? I wouldn't bet on it, way they're falling down around here."

"This thing does seem to have its own momentum."

It got quiet for a while so my cell flashed up a number I'd been anticipating all day. Not anticipating impatiently, nor really looking forward to—just anticipating.

I coaxed the phone to life, went: "S'up, big man?"

Trevor said, "Felix wanted me to call. He was wondering if you found anything out."

"Yeah? How about you? You wondering too, or was it just Felix?" Kidding him.

"Yeah, well, yeah. Me too. How bout it?"

"I believe I know who. Now I gotta figure out why."

"Why do you gotta find out why?"

"Cause that's how they wrote the rules, T. I'm with you: I think the motivation thing is way over-rated. But they didn't consult me when they were writing the rules."

Raleigh looks over, his face crazing into a puzzle. I grinned sideways at him.

Trevor: "Who is he?"

"I gotta sit on that till I'm sure, dog. Hang tight—it's rolling now. Won't be long."

"You tell the police so they can arrest him?"

"Not how it works, Trev. I gotta have more than just Harry-told-Sally when I go see them. Chill, enjoy your new toy."

"Okay. Cool. Uh..." He'd run out of dialogue.

"I'll call, kiddo. Be looking out for me."

"Okay. Can I still call you if I wanna?"

"Course you can, dog. Couple of anarchists like us gotta stay in contact."

We did byes.

Raleigh said, "Thought you were chatting with Booker for a minute." Being nosey.

"Was the president of Mensa. They're hounding me to join again."

It stopped there, Raleigh respecting my telling him it was none of his fucking business who it was. Truth? It was his business as much as mine now. I just figured one of us bumbling around in his sullied suit of armor trying to rescue matronly TV addicts and tweenagers was plenty. Things went quiet again for a bit.

Raleigh popped the muffle, said, "Know what, dog?"

"Yeah. I think I been watching the cups instead of the pea."

Raleigh nodded. "I'm just saying..."

"I hear you. Drop me at Miz Johnson's, lemme get my ride so I can shut my eyes for a minute. I got things to see and people to do tomorrow."

[26]

Awoke with the same old nag who'd kept me tossing most of the night: the key. There's always a door and always a key to it. I'd been to the rodeo enough I knew trying doors was nothing but folly. So what you found the right one if you didn't have the key to get beyond it? And I knew Rennie had the key. Had to. Who else could?

Of course Boris knew. Maybe Iveta. I didn't want her to, but I was losing foundation with her.

But it was Ren I had to see, see if I couldn't figure Boris's play, get out in front of the game. And there was a *game.* And Rennie *was* going to enlighten me.

Caught some federal highway fern-bound. Most of the hour's drive I spent telling myself: you rested well, try tact and patience while you're in the mood. Nice try—the closer I got, the less tactful and patient I felt. Come on Rennie, let's don't do this the hard way, please.

Journey's end, I hung a left and put my ride under what looked like the same live oaks as last visit. Watched the same berry-brown children play with the same gray dirt.

This morning the kids had a pig about Pomeranian-size. It was a fat little Poland China and when no one had a hand on him, he'd run for his life. The kids would run him down and he'd squeal nonstop till they let him go again. And he'd run.

My little friend from Texas was waist-deep in the flora again, about the same place.

"*Que pasa,* Tex?"

"S'up, pardner?"

"What, you work twenty-four seven now?" It was Sunday morning.

"Gotta couple a things working I needed to check on." He looked at himself. "Yeah, I gotta move, get ready to go to mass. Got us a *quinceñera* this afternoon too. I'd sooner be here as either one."

"Me too. Lemme guess: McAllen."

He stood, rubbed some humus off his hands, grinned a set of south Texas teeth at me. "Not bad, Deacon. Little dog-squirt between there and Laredo. Zapata. Know it?"

Yeah, I knew it. I knew all the southeast Texas border towns—Brownsville, Laredo, Rio Grande City, Zapata, McAllen. I could go on. Snuck pick-up campers full of dope through all of them one time or another.

"Café de Tomas still on the main drag there?"

The old dude smiled. He'd clued. "Un-huh. And out-a-towners still come in there for the same thing."

"The guided tour to Mexico, through the back door, huh?"

"The dry season specialty there. Some things never change." He grinned his sketchy grin at me, said, "Yeah, I sorta figured you for the Café Tommy type."

Funny. Some things never change. "My man in his lab?"

"He's back there somewhere. Hey, Deacon, can I ask you something?"

"Sure."

"The hell's going on around here?"

"Whadda you mean?"

"Didn't much change when Mr. Alvarez bought out the crackers that owned the place before—well, the pay got better. Then all these young bloods packing fancy heat begin running around here, now you show up. And I don't know who the hell you are or why you're here, or why you're always toting." He shook his *campesino's* hat. "But I know something's going on."

"I'm an old friend of Rennie's."

"I know that. But you tote. Look, Deacon, I know what Mr. Alvarez is into. I work with him in the stealth lab, I'm going to Canada with him, okay? But..." His hands were out; they wanted an answer. "Gun toting friends showing up? That's why I left south Texas, Deacon."

I dug in a pocket, found foldables.

I was going to give him a C to play along, but came out with three or four. I took his hat off his head, tucked the money in the sweatband and put the hat back where I found it. Then I watched him watching me.

"Somebody's wiped out Rennie's grow houses, killed some folks, killed a Seminole County parole officer Rennie was seeing."

He winced at that one.

"They tried setting Rennie up to pop him. Some reason, someone wants Rennie Alvarez dead."

The leathery little man was solemn, lower lip pinched pensively between thumb and neighbor. Little of that, a nod. A beat and a half. A: "Thanks, Deacon. That's white of you."

"Can I ask *you* something?"

"Sure, Deacon. Shoot."

"When did I get to be a deacon?"

The sketchy grin, the boney shrug. "Every time you show up, I go to praying."

"Yeah? Why's that?" Having fun.

"Cause I've killed men myself and my grandmother read bones. I can see you, Deacon." He was morbidly serious.

Some mutual whatever-it-is exchanged. There was nothing left to say so I said: *Bye.*

Nate the gunsel was on his stool by the tool-rack door. I never slowed, put out a fistful on knucks, got back knucks, used the sneaky door.

Skunk's ass, bat-shit and worm poo. That was the common smell to Rennie's empire. When he was working there add solvent smells, ether, ester or ketone smells. Today add the pungent odor of very good pot burning.

Mad Doctor Dank, the seed king, sat in a tall bar chair, leaned back, chilling, savoring, his feet on the stainless table. He toked, held it out to me.

I studied it as it smoldered between Rennie's fingers.

He exhaled, said, "C-99. The original Brothers Grimm, F-fucking-One generation, Sloan. Tastes like a pineapple smoothie. Makes you wanna conquer the world. All cerebral. No narcotic, no couch-lock. Stellar ride. Green crack. The Holy Grail of marijuana. Try it, old buddy."

Tact and patience—remember? Steady, Sloan.

I took the offered joint, kicked one of the two legs his stool was using. Ren hit the concrete floor pretty hard and I sucked on his high-test reefer.

I held the hit until Ren started stirring. I exhaled, said, "Dog, you get up, I'm gonna kick your fucking ass up past your fucking shoulders."

So he groaned. So he said, "You hurt me, Sloan."

So I go: "Wanna hit. I hear pot's a great general analgesic."

"The fuck's wrong with you?"

I hit the reefer, hoping it would knock the sharper corners off my desire to beat Rennie down.

Nope. Had to rely on my flimsy self-control.

I put the joint on the stainless table, deep huffed a few times, sat Rennie's chair up, grabbed him by his lab coat and put him in the chair. None of it was done charitably.

I put my face in Rennie's. "Rennie, you're gonna tell me about Boris and what it is you got makes him wanna kill you. And you're gonna tell me whose fucking side your wife's on. But Ren, mostly, I want you to tell me why you quit caring about people. Baby, you used to be beautiful. The fuck ever happened to you?" And, God forgive me, I slapped him outta the chair again.

Nate stuck his head in and I told him we were good. Told him to keep everyone out. He looked at Rennie on the floor, looked at me, hesitated.

I said: "Everybody includes you, Nate."

He withdrew and I put Rennie back on the stool, tried some more deep breathing. Rennie remained prudently mum.

"Talk to me, Ren." I picked up the Cindy roach, resparked it, babied it up, gave it over to Rennie. "Tell me the story, Rennie, or I swear to God I'll beat you fucking senseless."

I sat and we all watched wounded Rennie finish his Cinderella-99, F-fucking-One reefer and pout. He shuffled around to an ancient fridge, found us a couple of very cold Smithwicks, popped them, sat again. Trying me I guess.

I wouldn't clink when he held his bottle out. He grinned, shook his head.

"Okay, Sloan, start where?"

"Where you met your wife and her brother. I believe it'll flow from there."

Rennie sat a bit, collecting his memories, said, "Met Boris first. I hired him to deal with security issues when I was having some troubles, prior to the Janie thing."

"I see. Why'd you lie to me about it?"

He missed it going in his ear but caught it when it bounced off the inside of his skull. "Oh. That was another time. I was talking about this time. Didn't see it mattered."

"You're a terrible liar, Ren. I wish you'd stop. Where'd you get Boris?"

"One of my growers knew him, or of him."

Un-un. "Tell me it wasn't Gene in Narcoossee."

"Matter of fact. Why?"

"Don't worry about it. What sorta prior troubles did you experience, exactly, this other time?" Could see this falling together.

"Same as now, but not as serious. No one died. They just smashed up some places, kicked some people around, trashed the grows."

"Gene's place get smashed?"

"Yes."

"He get beat?" No.

Rennie thought. "No. No he didn't. Damn, Sloan, you think?"

"I'd not be surprised."

Rennie said, *Fuck*, started attacking a cell phone.

"If you're calling Gene, you're gonna get some serious roaming charges. Gene the teen-fucker's dead as boy-bands, baby."

Ren tossed the phone. I suggested he continue even though I could pretty well see where we were going. Sounded like some gen-u-ine, old-country cash-or-crash extortion, an east European specialty. Right up there with kidnapping and revenge killing.

"Well, bash Boris if you want, Sloan. He stopped the fuckers."

"I bet. He say who it was?"

"Yeah. Black guys."

"Of course it was." It always is. "Oh, Rennie, Rennie, Rennie. Then his sister happens to show up from the mother-land."

"No. I flew her over. She was in a bad situation—a government job and a high-level politico boss who was putting sexual demands on her. Bad situation."

Politico? Right. "It's a wonder she wasn't tied to the railroad tracks. Jesus, Rennie, how fucking stupid can you get?"

His hands came out in innocence but I didn't believe them. He said, "Sloan, I was just helping someone out."

Lying-fuck Rennie. "Why?"

"*Why*? What *why*?"

"Boris was gonna do what for you beyond this *security*?"

A halting hand, palm at me. "Sorry, Sloan. Company business."

I laughed. It was the most sincere thing I'd done in days. "Come on, Ren. You already look like a chump. Fess up."

Rennie deflated like someone pulled the stem out of his air valve. "Money."

I watched as he found his cutesy gnome pill vial, shook himself out a few, chased them with beer.

"You figured you married his sister, you could trust him to take your money by the laundromat. Oh, Jesus, Rennie. How much did he take you for?"

"He actually moved three to Canada to the new corp up there." He lost more wind from already slack sails. "But there's another six he's playing hide the cake with. He needs me personally to move it and he's not smart enough to figure out how to do it. Yet."

"But he's working on it?"

"Yeah."

"And it's all out in the open now? That he's fucking you? That his sister married you to fuck you?"

"Yeah."

"Jesus, Rennie, you make all that scratch from selling buds?"

The pills were smoothing him, cooling his eyes. "Some. Most, I guess. Both my trust funds matured when I turned thirty. I got a couple of mil outta that." He drifted a bit, came back, said, "I sell a lotta dope, Sloan, and I sell a lotta stuff that makes it grow. I grossed nearly three mil last year, just cannabis sales."

Tax free, I'm sure—that's why he needed a Boris. "So you let Boris bore his way into your pocket." I put on a perplexed face. "Why, Ren?"

"I was swamped, dude. The move to BC, this particularly elusive linalool terpene in these new migraine genetics I'm trying to dial in. And now, my website's exploding—two thousand hits a day in legal goods. On the down-low side, baby-boomers are rediscovering pot, Sloan. You can't keep the shit in stock. And, in spite of legalization here and there, prices keep going up."

"How nice for you. Was Boris the one giving you bad advice?"

"Yeah. I figured you showed up, he'd drift."

Right. "You still listening to him, Rennie?"

He came in from the cold, looked at me and lied. "Hell no." Then he laughed again. In the pocket, pull out the vial, decide against it, hide the vial.

"You're crazy as a bedbug anymore, aren't you, Ren?"

"There are several shrinks that would concur with that diagnosis, doctor."

"What're you taking?" *Gobbling* would be more descriptive.

"Sloan, I'm on four different anti-depressants, and still smoke a half-gram of bubble hash every night to sleep." Stupid grin. "I've self-prescribed myself a couple of oxy nineties a day. For the nerves. And I got nerves. You've met Boris and Iveta. They're like a nerve virus. I need a new pill."

"You need more than a new pill, Ren. What's wrong with you, really?"

Rennie puzzled up like he'd never thought about it. He caught a stray strand of reality, looked at me with the eyes of a drowning man. He said, "I don't know."

"Whadda the shrinks say?"

Back into the ether with a grin. "*Say*? Shrinks don't *say*. They watch your mouth move for an hour then charge you three bills for being polite. No, Sloan, all the king's Jungs and all the king's Freuds can't put Rennie Alvarez together again."

"Whadda you think it is, Ren?"

A distant shrug, a smaller voice: "I don't know. Somewhere along the line things changed. I don't even know when. All I know is that I don't feel anymore. No highs, no lows. No joy, no sorrow. No blacks, no grays—no color. Flat white, Sloan." Again, the drowning eyes. "Like the inside of my grow rooms, my whole life's flat white." Back to smiling Rennie, go in the gnome vial, toss a few pills. "Yep. I've become a fucking mess, Sloan."

"So you call me, fuck my life up."

He didn't care—he was gliding. "Come on, Sloan. I'm a fucking nerd. You're a genuine tough guy. You always win, always get what you want. You'll figure out how to lift this curse and get rid of these fuckers."

It was a little early for a beer for me so I drained the Smithie in one mass visit. I looked at the bottle, decided it was decent beer but there was too much writing on it. Said, "You realize all they gotta do is kill your ass and *all* of it's theirs."

"Not without my numbers it isn't." He seemed pleased with himself throwing a checkmate on Boris's stylings.

"They're gonna kill you eventually, Ren."

"Yeah, but they can't get away with it."

"Why's that, Ren?"

"Because I brought you on board, old chum." Some over-cooked smugness came with it.

I laughed some more. Maybe it was the Cindy. No—this shit was funny. "Ren, they'll just kill both of us."

More smug. "But you won't let that happen."

"You take a lot for granted, Rennie. Why don't you just leave?"

"Will you leave? Why should I?" A too-happy laugh. "For six mil?" A shrug. "They'd find me anyhow, Sloan, you know they would."

He was right. So I said, "Two hundred grand. Cashier's check. Tomorrow morning."

The man never flinched, so I said, "Better make it two-fifty."

I was losing him. I thought about slapping the shit out of him, but tried something else. "Why do you think Boris killed Janie Wall?"

It reined him in. "Boris didn't kill Janie."

"Of course he did, Ren. But why?"

I could see him working it hard, so I believed he truly didn't know. He said, "Why would he kill Janie?"

Is there and echo in here? "Unless I'm crazy as you, I'd say it was somehow over your money. Who'd you think killed her?"

He shrugged, slipped into the ether. "I was busy. I never thought about it much."

Okay, I could believe that. "If you've got the secret numbers to the cash, why was Boris trying to kill you at the rest area?"

He was chemically foggy, but he came back a bit, went confused. "What? Boris would be crazy to kill me before he knew the password. Why?"

"Don't know if you don't know, Ren. Maybe he's tired of fucking with you and is gonna settle for the three mil in BC."

"How could he manage that?"

"It's called inheritance. Remember your little wife? It'll all be hers—and Boris's."

He nodded then he was gone, off in that Never-Never-Land Rennie Alvarez's mind exists in. A world of terpenes and trichomes, clones and lumens, pH and RH, light cycles and feeding schedules, green sand and coco coir and F-1 Cindies.

If I could keep him alive long enough, they might give the nerdy fuck the Nobel.

[27]

The old Bolingbroke gal was ambling some, but it seemed as though she was moving towards our home. I gave her her head for a bit until I admitted I wasn't fooling anyone but myself. I was gonna deliver for the Wall kids, so what Rennie was a freak and a pill head anymore? This thing had moved beyond Rennie and his commerce. Nothing but point A to point B now.

I pointed the Shark's nose at the Belarusians. Why not? I've talked my way into tighter spots.

Sure, there are always rules and protocol with these people. You fuck up, you could end up with your nuts hanging on your mother's doorknob.

Had no mother. My nuts had never done anything but get me in trouble and spend my money. And I certainly had no regard for either rules or protocol.

Just walked up, tried the bohunk-clubhouse door. Locked.

Wait, someone was beckoned by my attempt. A short heavy guy in a short sleeved white shirt opened the door, asked, "What you want?" English would never be his first language.

"I wanna see the old man."

He surveyed me, appraised me, put me on a bit. "Who?"

The little guy had hard black eyes and I think he was used to cowering people with them. I watched my silhouette in them while he looked at my eyes.

Not sure what he found but he asked, "You got guns?"

"Yeah, but only one on me."

"You give to me?"

"Fuck no, I won't give to you."

We spent a few more beats pondering the abbreviated dialogue and its intrinsic meanings. All considered, the doorman says, "You got balls, buddy. Maybe you can wait a minute."

"Maybe you can hurry. I got a pedicure scheduled in an hour." Got a grin and a glass door in my face.

Short wait then a tall sideburns, forties, bothered, impatient, clicks the lock, opens the door.

"What?"

"You're not who I asked for."

"The fuck you want him to know?" Better English than the door monkey.

"I want him to know I don't fuck with flunkies. He and I got mutual problems. You understand mutual problems?"

"I was born in County Regional, Mr. Sloan." Telling me a few things at once.

"Good for you. What's his name?"

Some deciding. I thought no, but: "Demetree Dragonovitch."

I nodded. "Demetree the Dragon. So Demetree's Belarusian?"

"You've heard of him?"

I shrugged. "It's my niche. I have to know."

A nod, a: "Wait a couple of minutes, Mr. Sloan. Demetree wishes to speak with you as well. Do you like ice cream?"

"Love it."

"Good. Wait a moment please."

The door clicked shut and I wasn't sure what the last part meant exactly.

★★★

Always been a pistachio-almond devotee, with pistachio-pistachio being an undeniable reward for achieving nirvana when you can find it.

Demetree Dragonavitch found it for me four units down from his lair.

He'd come out like one of the old movie moguls, long thin trench coat draped over ample shoulders, crush Homburg perched on his broad head, about three grand worth of suit so conservative it could put the kibosh on a funeral, glistening cordovan wingtips to finish.

Before he acknowledged my existence, he read the weather, passed the long frail coat back to the second guy I'd spoken to. His man spoke some stuff I didn't get, Demetree said some back, his man and the frail coat drifted back into the clubhouse.

We strolled, not a care on the fucking planet for Dozen-Killer Sloan and Demetree the Dragon. Unintroduced. Couple of cool cats waiting the other out.

Either we'd have ice cream and a chat or we'd shoot at each other on the sidewalk here.

Kept him on my left side, ice cream in that hand till he said, "Thank you for not killing my grandson. He deserved it. Thank your dark friend as well for me."

"I'll do it. Kids, huh?" I licked in relief, but kept the Dragon on the left.

"You have them?"

"Yeah. Two. Two different moms."

Demetree winced at my foolishness, went sideways. "Can I ask if you know of three of our young men in the trunk of a car?"

Ouch. "I was the one left them in crack town. Sorry, but somebody left them in my front yard." I didn't mention it was Boris.

We walked, ice creamed.

"But you and your dark companion did not kill them?"

"No, sir. But I did watch them try to shoot a friend of mine at a rest area west of town."

Walk. Lick.

Demetree says, half question, half disgusted statement: *Boris.*

"I'd bet. Why? What'd they do?"

"We believe they were doing business with this animal. We hear they turned the game on this man Boris. It is unclear exactly what happened, but it seems they decided they wanted a bigger share of this business. You say the business was shooting at a friend of yours—you say shooting *at* so I hope he is okay." He shrugged, licked, said, "Our young men are learning bad habits in this country, each trying to be a bigger man than the next." Another shrug, another lick. "It seems as if they walked into a hornet's nest and died for their mistake." A shrug. "Even if it was the mistake of these three young men, they are our young men and my community will expect measure for measure." Some quiet—if it was acting it was good acting. Then: "It would seem we have developed a common enemy, Mr. Sloan. Maybe we should exchange telephone numbers."

Demi found a card, blank but for a handwritten ten digits, in an inner coat pocket. I reciprocated with my own nearly-blank card.

Man, I love sugar cones and new friends.

"Demi, tell me about this Boris fellow."

We walked in QT until our cones were nothing more than sticky fingers.

Then: "Why should I?"

"It might help me some day."

"Are you going to kill him?"

I shrugged. He wasn't looking at me but he still got it.

"Then I will tell you who this character is." A few steps, he looks me in the face, stops me with a beefy hand. "And you will never say Demi Dragonavitch tell you nothing. Deal?"

"Deal."

I put a hand out and the Dragon grabbed it so quickly and with so much gusto it caught me cold. You can shake hands with the devil in a lotta ways, but it's always a fucking rush.

[28]

Same scat Raleigh had: Boris was a life-taker. Life-takers are scary. Motivated life-takers are double scary. But, then, government sanctioned life-takers make the rest of the choir look like victims of circumstance—the sanctioned do it because they enjoy it.

Demetree's Iveta: she was a beautiful whore Boris pimped from his cop's perch back home. No, they weren't brother and sister. Just a whore and her pimp with me playing the John.

I left Dragonovitch pretty sure I could get him up to a hundred grand and I figured Raleigh could jack the Rooskies a little higher. Add Ren's quarter ton and I might could buy Guyana, Belize, somewhere like that.

Why not? I was gonna have to do Boris anyway. He'd demand it, make it a me-or-he situation. I wasn't good in those situations—I'd kill your ass like so pronto you wouldn't fucking believe it.

I'm thinking, *good luck, Boris,* sitting in Demetree's parking lot and there's Boris putting his pretend-brother-in-law's Escalade in a spare slot.

I stood up, out of my car. Boris saw me, grew a handgun so I did too.

I said, "Stay away from Rennie. Stay away from me. You don't, I'll kill you, Boris."

"I have business with him."

"Un-huh. But did you see him walk off from a three-mil-a-year grow business, dumb-ass?" I shrugged. "He walks off, grows the Canadian thing up? Come on, legalization's on us. It's gonna be big biz. Six measly mil? Rennie'll let it sit till it rots. Go suck it, Boris."

Sorely thought the fuck was gonna lift and throw. He stood down, so I did too. Shit, I was being totally amenable today for a prison-certified psychopath. My karma graced my efforts—Dragonovitch opened the clubhouse door, stepped out. He said something in his tongue that made Boris want to kill me and Demi both.

He didn't. He got in his brother-in law's Cad and left.

Demetree says, to me, "We are now even."

I laughed, said, "Not even close, but thanks for the lift." I eased a little peace sign at him.

He conceded with a smile and a wave. "When you kill him we must have an ice cream and you can tell me how you did it. I'm old—my only joys are vicarious. Sleep light—he knows tricks you may not."

The guy still standing in the parking lot with a pistol in his hand said, "Thanks for the warning," and he got in his Vette and went home. He needed to run some Hoppe's through his hardware.

***

Had Raleigh on my shoulder, pushing greasy cleaning wads through nine millimeter barrels.

Raleigh said: "My Russian goes looking for current grease on your boy Boris. News is in. Could be Boris's still a cop over there looking into his countrymen over here, supposedly. If you care."

So I said nada. I'd heard the same from my ice cream buddy.

So Raleigh says: "You hearing me?"

"Un-huh." Yes, Raleigh, I heard. Just didn't have much of a come-back.

"So whatchu gonna do, bread?"

I said nada some more.

Raleigh said, "I see. He plans on bringing company when ya'll do it, lemme know. I got your back, baby, you need."

"I know you do, brother. Thanks. See you."

I killed the phone. Raleigh had more but I was somewhere else. I didn't need company where I was. I was a one-man show now.

Suicide, accident or balls-up cold-blood. I had to take one of those hideous sisters to the dance. Which would it be?

No one would believe that pain-in-the-ass, narcissistic Boris would off himself. Plus, too much planning and plotting and conniving.

Accident? Here again way too much of the tactical and strategical, decently moderate conniving but harboring the ever troubling *accidental* witness possibility.

Cold-blood it was. Nothing but a bit of conniving and bang-bang with that one.

Packed up some hardware and some underwear and headed for my staked goat, my bait, my dog Rennie. I figured you got a live Rennie that's worth somewhere between three and nine mil dead, the Borises of the world will come to the bait.

Caught the Four, knowing the federal concrete would get me to the fernery faster than the romantic back roads.

I hit the big bridge at the St. Johns, my cell chirps. I miss it but catch the rest area bottom of the bridge.

Park. Caller ID says Iveta. I punch her up.

She hellos me. She's been crying. I think, or I was being played to think.

"S'up, doll?"

"I am so glad I caught you. Can you come over?"

"No, sweetheart. I gotta go see your brother the jackal doesn't eat your husband the jackass."

She cried into the phone for me. I didn't respond as though I was buying the drama. My my, look at me.

"He beat me."

"Who? Boris?" Buying in, Sloan. See yourself, buying in, asshole?

"No. Renaldo."

Please—Ren wouldn't beat his meat, much less a wife. So I go: "Yeah? Why?"

"He is drunk and high on his pills. Now he is in the library with a bottle of scotch and a revolver. He says he is tired of life."

Shit. Why me?

"Give him the phone."

"No. Please, Duncan, please come. He is crazy drunk. He crashed into the gates when he arrived. Now he is in there pointing the gun around."

A noise, maybe a bang. Who knows?

"Oh God, he has shot himself."

Then the phone bumped around and Iveta screamed her way out of earshot.

Oh my.

If it was theatre, goddam, it was damn good stuff.

Dialed Ren. No live Ren—got mechanical Ren.

Me: "Dad, you need to call me like first break you get. If you aren't home drunk, lock your Castilian ass in your lab till I get to you." Second thoughts. "Better yet, get in that Italian piece of shit car of yours and get far, far away. Call."

Three minutes out, Iveta rings me back.

"Hey."

"He is gone, Duncan."

Some juice heated my face and belly up. "Gone dead or gone driving?"

"Driving."

I blew my relief at the windshield, held the phone away some.

Then: "Where'd he go, doll?"

"I did not see him. He was gone when I got downstairs."

"He take the gun?"

"No, it is on his desk. Please come here."

Man I could feel the fence biting into my crotch.

Was she or wasn't she?
Would she or wouldn't she?
Why not let your dick decide, Sloan?

[29]

Celled up Nate the high-yellow gunsel. He told me how he'd not seen anyone non-Mexican since Rennie'd left. Said that was shortly after I buzzed out. Said Rennie said he had to run home, would be right back. Then the Mexican Army had gone to mass, so now Nate was there on his lonesome. Should he come in to town?

"No. Sit tight. Rennie's on the wing so he'll probably come there. I'll be there in a bit. Call me if he shows." I tossed the phone on the other seat.

Shit.

I said it again: *shit.*

Right there, after being told she was a whore, a liar and a thief, with instincts clanging like a wind-chime factory, a sane man woulda saddled up, chased the sunset down. No, I floated on a nano-particle of hope, wanting something that wasn't. I floated up until I could see myself. I watched from above as my old patched-up Vette turned around, headed for hell. Through the sunroof, the guy driving looked like a nice enough fellow—made me wonder how he kept getting himself into shit like this.

I got back in the car with him and it seemed crowded.

Some concrete, some asphalt, some street lights then stop signs and I got to see Rennie's iron gates strewn across his driveway.

I hobbled my ride on the street, got out and dragged a gate half out of the drive and onto the lawn.

Back in the car after dusting hands on ass, re-hobbled on the pink pavers.

Some kind soul had finally put plywood over the door where somebody had smashed it out with his nine-millimeter sidearm. The door was polite and surrendered to my keylessness.

No sound.

My bristling parts bristled. I pulled, scoped.

Nada.

"Iveta." A question, really, but the real question was did Iveta set me up for a lead party with Boris and his goons.

Nada.

I went from casual carry to I'll-shoot-your-ass, gat up in both hands. Eased in. Called again. Some quiet answered. My nipples were so tight I could feel them.

The hall or the stair?

The stair—don't know why.

I glided up, back to the wall, eyes wide, piece ready. The quiet got deafening—there was way too much of it—so I shouted.

A moan? Did I hear a moan?

Fools rush in, me right there with them as a rule. No rules broken, I kicked Iveta's bedroom door open in a full charge, the Nine way out in front daring the felonious world.

Iveta exits the bath with one eye black; we're both sporting astonished faces.

She was nearly naked but my gun arm went flaccid anyway.

"Jesus. Didn't you hear me call?"

"No. I was in the shower, darling."

The scene revolved and she was in my arms, I had a towel pulling her in.

We made the bed and I took the towel away, lay on her. Gat still in hand, I rose to my knees, pushing her legs open.

So my cell has to make noise, ruin the special moment. Woulda let it complain but I was looking for a Rennie. Fished the phone from a pocket, got a Paulie.

I looked down at what lay squirming below me, wondered had pervish Paulie managed to bore into my brain and was calling to confirm what he was seeing.

Me: "S'up?" Pause, watch Iveta move under me. "What concourse?"

Pause, watch. "I'm busy right this red-hot. Lemme run. See you in a half hour." Dumped Paulie, moved my eyes up the fine body to Iveta's eyes. I grinned like things were funny.

Response: "Fuck me, Duncan. Fuck as you wish, where you wish. I find you... What is it called? Irresistible?"

"I'd call it bullshit. Tell you what, sweetcakes, I'd take a ride but I gotta go grab a lawyer at the airport, see if he can figure out how to keep my ass outta jail."

"What have you done for jail?"

More grinny grin. "Nothing much yet, but stick around."

"Why are you smiling like this, Duncan? It is making me uncomfortable."

I said, "You got me, didn't you?"

She went innocent. "Whatever do you mean, my darling?"

I gently caressed the side of her noggin with the muzzle of my piece, said, "If Boris is off killing Rennie right now, you better run hide, bitch."

She slapped me full on, told me I was a fool. Told me to get off her.

"Who hit you in the eye?"

"Get out of here, you fuck. Can you hear me?"

"Boris? He the one left you smelling like fish?"

I'd had my fun. I got off, left.

I didn't wanna hear any of the answers to any of my questions.

★★★

The great anonymous *they* tell you what happens in Vegas stays in Vegas.

Guess Paulie didn't get the memo.

I pull into the pick-up lane under suspicious cops' eyes and there's short Paulie gabbing at a set of forty-two, forty-four quad-D's he coulda suckled from flat-footed. And I mean it when I say he was gabbing at the quad-D's. For all Paulie cared, the woman could have looked like Dick Nixon—he wasn't planning things for her face. Wait now, we're talking Paulie here. Nothing's outta play in Paulie-World—nothing.

I nose in, honk, get a crumpled face from Paulie. I get it: if Jugs is with Paulie we got a problem. Two seats, three asses. If the big suitcase sitting curbside was hers then we had more problems, and it wouldn't be the hideous floral pattern either.

Paulie brings his crumpled face at me, and check it out. Yep, Betty Boop's trailing behind him, pulling the sofa-sized luggage piece like a barge.

Paulie leaned in, goes: "Why'd you come get me in this piece a shit?"

"Sorry, Paulie, the Fleetwood's in for its fifteen mile maintenance. See that yellow car right there, sign on top. It's called a cab. Raise your hand and one of them will be happy to meet your every need." I head wagged at the chippy. "New wife?"

Paulie made a face. "Hell no."

"What? She find out you're short and spend all your scratch on titty-bars and going to Vegas?"

"Fuck off. She's never been to the theme parks. I told her I'd show her around."

"You should take her to Ripley's. She'd probably get in free."

"Funny guy, Sloan. Somebody should get you a microphone and a laugh track. How're we gonna work this?"

★★★

Turns out, her name was Loretta and she was smarter than you'd hope someone with a blow-up doll's figure would be. She was smart enough to get Paulie's cheap ass to fly her in and was already asking how far it was to Miami.

Paulie was in her lap—they'd tried the converse and Paulie couldn't take it. Her big floral wardrobe was bungeed to my sketchy luggage rack and I expected any minute to look back and see luggage, luggage rack and all bouncing down the highway.

I merged, said, "Three, four hours. You got friends in Miami?"

"Yes." Nothing more.

Made me smile which made Paulie turn and try to look Loretta in the face.

It was tough on him. His eyes were going up and down like a couple of bolo paddle balls. "Who do you know in Miami?"

She mustered her strength for a shrug, said, "Nobody much. A couple of friends. I thought I might rent a car and drive over there in a day or two."

I, picador, said: "What about those theme parks?"

She hugged Paulie into her ample bosoms, said, "Ah, who needs those old silly theme parks? I got my own little Mickey right here." And pulled Paulie's ears out.

Paulie wasn't so easily distracted by a flank move. He said, "When're we going to Miami?"

"Oh, sweetie britches, I'm not gonna trouble you anymore. I'll just get my return flight changed to Miami International." Sounding a bit premeditative like maybe she'd pulled this trick before.

Man, the grin was crawling all over my face. Here's the deal, Paulie: couple of days with those snow-capped peaks of Loretta's or be the ass and watch her drop you like she'd drop a...well, a little short, bald, perverted motherfucker.

Paulie was working it but I knew where he'd end up. "I'm not paying for the transfer, though."

"I don't expect you to, sweetie. My friend in Miami said he would."

Paulie's lame come-back: "Well, alright then. Good."

Looked like the details on who would be fucking Loretta and when were all worked out. Said, "Where to, Esquire?"

"My office."

"Cool." Couldn't wait to see Loretta's face when she walked in Paulie's little Washington Street office.

On a good day it smelled like the inside of a cane-cutter's Nike. It'd been closed up for a few days and I was sure the stench would be so palpable you could probably see it undulating in waves.

Caught a correct exit off the 408, bounce along some of our tragic brick streets, put the Shark on the curb. I watched the lovebirds de-car and grinned like a guy who hadn't slapped a close and dear friend around, had ice cream with a Slavic mobster or threatened to kill an Eastern-European cop so far today.

I was unbungeeing Loretta's suitcase while she was asking Paulie did he live here too. He said yeah, and I could hear Loretta grinding a day off Paulie's joy ride. Wait'll she gotta sniff of the inside. Poor Paulie.

I got the armoire rolling but held back to enjoy the moment in full frame.

Paulie jingled his keys, poked one in the deadbolt, twisted it, threw the door back, being the gentlemen.

Loretta and the twins breezed in then, get this, started gagging. She turned, the bulkhead that was her bosom mowed Paulie aside. Couple of more gags on the sidewalk, she began waving her hand in front of her face but didn't seem capable of speech yet.

She finally got out: "Dear Mother of God. What's that smell?"

Paulie said, "I musta forgot to take out the trash before I left. I'll open some windows, let some fresh air in."

Please. You could knock down one side of the place and not lose that funk. There were probably enough wharf rat pelts under Paulie's floorboards to do up fur coats for the entire Continental Army. Bye-bye, Loretta. Enjoy Miami, dear.

Paulie disappeared inside and windows began going up.

I parked Loretta's luggage, said, "Startling, isn't it?"

She looked at me, shook her head. "Honey, I grew up in a paper-mill town and I've never smelled anything like it. What is it?"

"Corruption. You want I should take your bag inside?"

She thought about it maybe a second, said, "No. Would you take me to a rental car place?"

"No, babydoll. Paulie's an odd little man but he's a friend of mine." And everybody knows I don't fuck around with my friends' women.

"I could make it worth your while."

"I'm sure you and the kids there could, but no thanks."

"You'd love them." She did a little shoulder-shift, presentation move for me.

"Already do."

"You know, some guys like to give them names, you know, like they give their junk names. Mr. Happy, Little Elvis, Doctor Johnson."

"Yeah?" I could hear Paulie's office answering machine telling him who'd called while he was in Sin City. "What's the best one you've heard?"

"One guy called them Mutt and Jeff. See the right one's bigger than the left one."

"Hmm. So you've got one big tit and one regular tit."

"No. I've got one big tit, and one magnificent tit. I pad the dinky one." And she squeezed it to show me how she'd pulled off the illusion. "What would you call them?"

"Probably Leftittia and Rightittia, but I'm not giving you a ride, doll."

She huffed at my inexplicable rejection, said, "Fine." She sat on her suitcase and dug around in her purse, fed her nicotine habit. I smiled, said, "Take care of the equipment and have fun in Miami."

"Don't you worry your pretty head, handsome. I always have fun. Too bad you don't."

I agreed and disappeared so she could too.

***

Pulled my T-shirt over my nose like a gang-banger getting ready to do the local 7-Eleven and found Paulie in his office chair moping.

I said, "Whadda you expect, Paulie? What's she? A show-girl, a stripper, a whore? What?"

"Yeah." All he had.

I let him pout for a few knowing his resilience would prevail.

He says: "You notice her hoots?"

I looked at him like he'd asked if I could build him a nuclear reactor from scrap iron. "Jesus, Paulie, would you notice if someone left Mount Rushmore on your front lawn?"

Paulie gave me some eyebrow action. "You mean Twin Peaks, don't you?"

It made me smile; I was glad the T-shirt was hiding my glee. I said, "You haven't fucked her yet, have you?"

"Of course I've fucked her." Pause to query. "Why?"

"Trust me. You haven't fucked her, and it's Mount Rushmore. Can we do some business now?"

I sat across the desk from Paulie in a client chair that had seen too many client fannies. I watched him review his notes for a bit, then watched over his shoulder as Loretta's tits snaked a ride out front from an optimistic opportunist in a conversion van.

Loretta, Mutt, Jeff and her floral-patterned prairie schooner loaded in a side door. The door slid shut and she was no more than another sad The-End in the continuing saga entitled *Paulie Mopes.*

Didn't mention it to Paulie: didn't want to sidetrack him from curing my current dilemma. I eased the T-shirt off my nose, tested. Bad, but not up there on the smelling salts scale anymore.

A few minutes, Paulie looks up, asks how much Booker knows.

"As little as I could tell him. He knows about the girl in the car firsthand. He knows about the parole guy. Told him about the rest area blow-down. He found the three bodies and tied the car to me and Raleigh." I thought some. "He might tie us to Fadi Korbani but I doubt it unless Nookie gets popped for something else and needs a deal. Haven't mentioned Demetree Dragonovitch or this Boris fucker. That's it: little as I could and stay on the street."

"Well, from my chat with him, don't make any plans for travel. He insinuated a warrant for accessory to improper disposal. Times four."

"He knows better than that. I only accessorized the first. The other three I straight out dumped. I asked you before: accessory to who?"

"That's *to whom.* He doesn't know who dumped the girl?"

"Un-un. Not for positive and neither do I, for *positive.* I gave him Rennie's name and address but he hasn't laid eyes on Rennie yet."

"So all he's really got are your prints on the Lincoln."

"I hope."

"And you haven't shot anyone but Korbani?"

"Right. So far."

Eyebrows arch. "So far?"

"That's why I'm sitting here, Paulie. This Boris fuck'll get us there. Give him time."

"Let's go after him, put him in sideways pinstripes. Can you prove he's killed anyone?"

"Paulie, please. The guy's a pro. Works for the government back home."

"You think he's got diplomatic cover?"

"He'd have to as bold as he seems to be."

I watched Paulie. He wasn't dumb.

He said, "You gonna shoot a diplomat now?"

"Whatchu want me to say, Paulie? I've been here before. I don't need a script to see what's breaking. And I'd like to consider it *have to* instead a *gonna.*"

He nabbed the phone, fingered the pad, waited. Said: "Lieutenant Booker, please, ma'am." Wait. Then: "Lieutenant, Paul Mopes. How are you?" Pause. "I see. I see. I see." Pause to look at me. "Yes. When I see him, I'll certainly tell him. Thanks." Drop the handset on its cradle.

"Booker's pissed, Sloan."

Really? "I coulda told you that before you put me on the timer. What'd he say?"

"He says you stumbled into a drug war and he's bringing you in for you own protection."

That was bullshit on so many levels I didn't even qualify it with a response.

"He wants *me* to bring you in." Made Paulie smile when he said it.

"I'd pay to watch that. He ask where I was?"

"No. I guess..."

I was up and moving. "Then we'll have to finish this up at a later date, Paulie. He'll be out front in a few minutes if you need to talk to him."

"Fuck Booker. I'll be talking to Loretta's twat by the time he pulls up."

I said, "Don't count on it. See you at my bond hearing."

***

Dialed Ren again. No Ren again.

Dialed Nate again. No Nate this go.

Dialed Iveta thinking she'd *maybe* tell me if she'd heard from Rennie. No Iveta.

Goddammit. I might as well be running around with a fucking windsock over my head. People kept falling down around me, and I was doing what? Nothing was what.

Goddammit.

I was pissed and I was the only jerk present to be mad at. So I did the mature, sensible thing—I took it out on the Vette, hoping for the chance to try on some back-water cop, see what his back-water road skills looked like under the cover of dusk.

No takers and I must have blown through six, eight burgs getting to Ren's house-of-fern.

Quiet as a bowling pin's sex life under the oaks. Dark as trouble and I knew that was wrong—my previous visits, I'd seen enough security lights that the place should be looking like a scene from *Apocalypse Now*.

I sat and listened to the quiet and watched the dark a while wondering once again in the same day was I being set-up for a lead party. Decided it was the perfect place for it.

The vibration and jingle from my cell made me jump a bit. I swung my vision across the murk, looked at caller ID.

Unfolded it, said, "What's shaking, T?"

"It's Felix, Mr. Sloan."

"Hey, Felix."

"Hi. Trevor said I could call. Is it okay?"

"It's fine."

"Trevor says you know who killed our mom."

"Maybe, Felix, maybe. Strong maybe. I'll call, okay?"

"Okay. Trevor wants to talk. Here."

Some fumbling, some male-sibling exchange, then, "Hello."

"How's it going? Use all your minutes up yet?"

"Nah. I text a lot but I got unlimited text. Can I ask you something?"

"Shoot"

Not what I'm thinking, he says, "Gramma says I gotta share the phone with Felix. Do I?"

Great. Okay, check the lay for moving shadows while I think about it. All I got, and it ain't King Solomon stuff: "Hey, dog, just to keep the peace, I'd give him ten minutes every hour. That's five to one. And tell him he can't hoard his minutes and hog the phone for an hour. He uses it or he loses it. How's that sound?"

"Alright, if I gotta share."

"Please."

"Alright. How's the other thing going? You know..."

"Yeah, I know. Closing in on this guy. Listen, I'm in the middle of nowhere in the dark. Lemme go right now."

"Okay. Will you call?"

"Bet on it."

A bit of quiet from the kid who quit believing in promises. Then: "Okay. Bye."

Man, I ain't cut out for that shit. No one's ever accused me of being a parent, and I know why— I feel nothing but clumsy and oafish when I try.

I watched the dappled dark a few more minutes, deciding should I do a flashlight-less, braille search of the place, and a pick-up rolled in, stopped. It backed-up a bit to put its lights on the darkened greenhouses. Moved forward, put its lights on me, flashed a couple of quick times. I semaphored my presence with a raised hand from the car's window.

The truck pulled to the side of the big house and stopped. Tex the Am-Mex got out, fussed in an ancient fuse box and got things glowing again.

I met him halfway. His outlook was grim to doubtful.

"This don't look good a'tall, Deacon."

The twilight was losing ground and that serious country-darkness was overwhelming us. "You got a flashlight, I know you do."

Unfortunately he did, so I went and found Nate by the two-gallon containers all leaked out.

No Rennie nowhere.

"Let's see what's going on in the lab, Tex."

Tex really didn't wanna and neither did I.

I took the light and eased the door open. I called out for Rennie, got nothing back but QT. I shined the light around. Nothing but more QT.

"Where's the switch?"

Tex came around me, fumbled on a wall and we had light.

A bit more of a mess than usual but mostly just more QT.

I said, "Let's go."

Tex hit the lights and we went out into the night.

I stood for a while looking at the sky. Had nothing. Handed Tex his flash, said, "What's your mama's magic telling you?"

He pondered some, told me: "Nothing. My brain's telling me they ain't no back door to the lab. If they went through the colored boy here..." Meaning Nate.

I pondered some.

"What kinda security we got? Cameras?"

"Some here and there. That ain't my deal. My daughter could show you but she ain't here. They's a room in the big house. Got some alarm stuff, recorders and such. Like I say..."

"I hear you, Tex." I fired my phone up, punched it with a digit. "Tex, I want you to see nobody comes back here, nobody goes in the big house. Got it?" Raleigh answered. "Hold on, dad. Tex, you hear me, right?"

"Yeah, Deacon."

"Good. Raleigh, we need to look at some security tapes."

"Why?"

"Might keep us outta jail."

"Where you at."

"Rennie's fernery."

"Umm-hmm. You make Booker's dozen yet?"

"Closing in. You got the fernery?"

"Gimme the address—I'll GPS it."

I relayed from Tex, folded the phone.

"Let's go look at this security room."

Tex shown the light on Nate. "What about him?"

"Me and my friend'll deal with him." Hmm—thinking what a resourceful little character Tex seemed like, I said: "Unless you can."

"No, no." Then he says: "What's it worth?"

"For him to disappear?" I shrugged out, "Five hundred."

"You particular?"

I thought about it, thought how I should feel something. I'd suggested Nate stay and wait on Ren, now he was dead. Maybe he was a gunsel and that's what happens to us gunsels sometimes. Or maybe I'd been spending too much time around Rennie Alvarez. "No."

"Care if he gets found or not?"

"No."

"Deal."

I shook Tex's rough hand on it and he showed me to the big house.

[30]

Raleigh's watching me watch the monitor was almost physical, meaning: I could feel it on the side of my face.

I played it straight-faced, robbed him his pleasure.

The main feature opened with a calming exterior shot of the fernery done in quiet. No nothing but trees and dirt and enslaved flora—no Mexicans, no gunsels, no mad scientists, no nobody. The quality was that shadowy, grainy security-cam shit. Lower right was a digital timer counting its ass off. It said: 02:21 and seconds.

Nice: just about the time Iveta called and turned me around on the interstate. Would've been very clever work if she'd been dealing with someone who thought from the dick less.

Raleigh says: "Here we go."

SUVs roll in frame. Okay, we'd seen SUVs. Sideburned punks get out. We'd seen punks. Hmm, Demi the Dragon's grandkid moving around like he'd hardly been shot in the gut recently. A doo-rag I'd seen before. If the fat white kid gets out, somebody should sing Auld Lang Syne cause the gang's all here. The SUV evacuates White-Boy—sing the song.

Then here's my Boris, walking on stage. Raleigh said, "Look here. S'up, my niggah? Where's your car?"

"Long walk from town, isn't it?"

"Brother Boris knows you can deny your face on this sketchy footage but not your tag number. You notice he ain't taking off his shades or looking at any cameras."

There was a little huddle, a little tête-à-tête. The ratty crew moved off.

I looked over at Raleigh. He told me to hold on, worked the mouse, selected a small screen from the bottom of the monitor. A view of the greenhouse that hid Rennie's lab came up. There's Nate still alive and well. There's our gang. Nate senses trouble, slides off his perch, hand in loose pants, on a gat I assumed.

Boris moves up aggressively on Nate as the eclectic crew fans out. Nate squares off with Boris, begins to pull, his head jerks forward. He tries to get his balance, goes limp, body swaying. A bit of spurting and Nate's not in the scene anymore. A couple of anonymous sideburners kick in the disguised door to Rennie's lab. The entire of the cast uses the door, leaving the view playerless.

Raleigh stopped it, said, "You see this, right?"

"Yeah." Why talk about it? Someone had slipped up behind Nate, head popped him, then they went in and did Rennie I suspected. I had a nice adrenalin leak going and my breath was deep and in cadence with my heart.

Raleigh fast forwarded through the vacant scene, stopped, went back a tad. Next, multi-talented Santos the doo-rag exited, came back with a forklift and a fifty-five gallon drum.

Santos wrestled the drum though the lab door and all was quiet again.

Raleigh zipped to the next piece of action, slowed on Boris exiting the lab. A few seconds, the crew comes through the door, Doo-Rag pulling a hand truck with the drum strapped to it, White-Boy on the drum's other end, humping.

The help loaded the drum onto the forklift's skids while the young sideburners burn Marlboros and act tough, polish their toe nails.

Doo-Rag mounts the lift, begins to back away and the monitor went blue.

I said, "Say why."

"Somebody deleted all the security files off the computer before they shut it down."

"What were we seeing?"

"Maybe that somebody didn't know they was a fifteen minute backup file constantly rolling over."

What am I saying? The fucking psycho's a goddamned genius, but if I react, praise him even mildly, I get charged more. So I go: "Cool. That's all you could come up with? That fifteen minute segment?"

"Fuck you, Sloan, you son of a bitch. You goddam caveman, you couldn't even a got the fucking main platform up and going."

"What's a platform?"

Raleigh watched me, read me. "Does it matter? Show's over. Would another fifteen minutes make it any different, dog?"

Checkmate. "No."

"And here's you one that's worse: what if that somebody *did* know they was a fifteen minute back-up?" Raleigh peeled a piece of art from under his right arm, poked it at me. Said, "Bread, these folks may be smarter'n you think they are. And they definitely tote better shit than you. Take it."

I shrugged at him. "I'm good. Familiar's better than fancy."

Raleigh sneered at *fancy.* "Humor me. Take it."

I took it.

"Here." Raleigh shucked a ring off a finger, hung it on his smallest for me. "You'll need that."

The ring was a plain signet job, *HK* in gold letters set in an onyx plateau. I slid it on my right ring finger. "Like this?"

"Just like that. Sloan, I'm gone tell you again, you want help you know all you gotta do is holler, but seems like you looking to take this thing home solo."

I had nada. Sat pat, so Raleigh looks over, says, "I said: seems like you looking..."

"I heard you, dad. You really wanna discuss what I gotta do?"

"Ain't nobody here but me and you, Sloan. I'm trying to ask are you sure on this thing."

"Wouldn't take much convincing at this juncture."

"But you don't *know* what was in that drum. How bout you shoot your friend's brother-in-law and your friend shows up. Say they *all* shamming you. Say your boy and the woman're trying to get rid of Boris."

There was wisdom in Raleigh's devil's advocacy, but I was running on instinct now. My senses told me Rennie was dead and I was gonna see Boris in a like condition.

"Well, let's go look in some barrels."

Raleigh wagged head, said, "You just humoring me, ain't you?"

"Weren't you doing the same?"

He thought about it, agreed he probably was. "What happens we *don't* find your friend?"

"I'll go see Dragonovitch, ask him why his grandson was on a video killing people."

"Where's that going? You looking for a blessing?"

"I guess—I don't wanna have to kill 'em all."

[31]

No Rennies alive or dead that Raleigh, Tex or I could find. Like I'd noted earlier: beyond a little disarray in Rennie's aerie—the lab—and a dead Nate, it was as if nothing had gone on.

We were cleaning up at a work sink attached to the side of the house, and when I was good and soapy my cell alerted. I rinsed, dried my hands on my pants and fetched up my phone. Missed the call by fractions.

My my. Look at this. A number I'd seen written on a card recently.

My palms prickled and moistened, my heart revved slightly and my breathing chased the beat. The adrenaline leak had begun again—I was approaching the killing zone now. I was in free-fall, floating through an atmosphere thick as chia fresca. I could feel it like I could feel my bones beneath skin and muscle.

I pushed recall. Waited for a voice. Said: "It's Sloan. The old man called."

The voice said, *Yeah.* Said, *Hold on.*

Demetree came on. "I need to see you."

"Yes, you do."

"You know?"

"Saw a movie about it."

"Can I buy you an ice cream, Mr. Sloan?"

"It's late, uncle." It had become tomorrow while we were looking for Rennies in barrels.

"I own the store. I want ice cream now, I get ice cream now. Can you come, Mr. Sloan?"

"If you make it pistachio-pistachio, and we drop the misters."

"Done. See you in how long?"

"Gimme an hour. I'm up the road a piece. Hey, Demi, how'd you hear? Your grandson tell you?"

"Eventually, my new friend. One of his stupid associates had to brag for killing the swarte and we hear about it."

"You hear what happened to my friend?"

"Come. We talk. I try to convince you not to kill my grandson."

I didn't respond so he said, "I have a trade I wish to discuss."

"See you at the ice cream joint."

I folded the phone, grinned at Raleigh. "I think I fucked right around, caught me a ride on a dragon."

"You always were a nimble motherfucker. Don't get your britches scorched."

"Always try not to." You couldn't have smeared the grin off my face with granny's double-action drawing salve.

★★★

One row of lights, a sleepy man in pajamas under his open black suit coat, Demetree Dragonavitch, a guy named Sloan. That was it.

Dragonovitch claimed a vinyl table and poked at his sugar-free in a cup like he didn't really want it. "We ask some people who is this man Duncan Sloan." He took a small, delicate nibble, poked some more. "The answers are... different. Depends who you ask. You could be a saint or a mercenary or a cold-blood killer, my friend." A shrug, a nibble, a poke. "Depends who you ask. But..." The little flat wooden spoon got poked at me. "They all, even those who say you are an assassin, respect you. I admire a man who can kill men and still have respect."

"It's a juggle. Look, Demi, I don't want your grandkid's nuts. I want Boris. I *would* like to hear what the kid has to say."

Demi leaned over, dropped the nearly full cup of ice cream in a waste bin, looked at a few grand worth of subtle wrist watch. "He is gone, in the air as we speak. I sent him to Canada for a while."

"Smart move. So what're we trading on now he's gone?"

"Boris's life. I give you one hundred thousand."

"Mind telling me why? I know some people who know you too, Demetree. You got tons of triggers. Why me?"

"If one of my people does this, the secret police will send someone to my community to see where is Boris. This is how we get Boris in the begin. No, no one from my community can have anything to do with it. We shall know nothing."

"I'm not hearing anything yet." I grinned, started in on my sugar cone, crunching the rim.

"From his predecessor, Boris get paper. This paper say I am someone else when I am very young. This someone is a wanted fugitive from our mother country. The paper is for extradition. At some point, this Boris man will either want money or my exile from this country—they all do."

Oh my. "I'll think on it."

"Please, do that. If you decide yes, give me details on your preferences for compensation. I will deliver this bastard up to you soon after you call."

"What about my friend? What did the grandson say?"

"I am sorry. He say he don't pull the trigger, but, honestly, my friend Sloan, I don't know I believe him. But—this is why I give you one hundred thousand. See, I know already you are going to kill Boris. The first time we meet, I see this in your eyes. So, another fifty for his head."

"The hundred large is ample. Like you say: me and Boris got future issues, no matter."

"No. You misunderstand, Duncan Sloan. I want his head. Just the man's head."

My cone broke down and dribbled green goo on the linoleum tiles. I watched it spread, buying time, assessing this new and interesting piece of the game.

"How would you suggest I deliver something like that?"

Dragonovitch smiled, said, "I do not care, but I would consider using something that did not leak and it should also be discreet."

Sound and prudent advice if I ever heard any.

***

So, if hearsay was proof, then Ren was dead. If Raleigh were here, he'd say what if Boris, Iveta, Rennie, Demetree Dragonovitch, his grandson and the entire of the Bohunk Club were all in concert, hinking me? How? For what? Who was I? What'd I do?

Sure, I had people hating on me. I'd put a few felonious fucks in slam. So what? Everybody's watched so much video at this juncture, we all think bad guys should be like Steven Seagal or somebody, twenty-pound chopper in his hands cutting cop cars in half with armor piercing rounds. Not. My bad guys are crack-heads and crank-heads and lazy motherfuckers who'll only get outta bed to cap someone for a shockingly scant return. Shit, Boris and Iveta were about as classy as recent memory would conjure. I was smaller than small potatoes—why pick on me?

Seemed like I was working my imagination to a frazzle so I let it all go. What went down went down. Was only life any-fucking-way. The Shark knew its way home from most anywhere you could name so I let 'er go. We sailed homeward, and at least one of us slept poorly.

That one woke late Monday morning, ground some dark beans, braved the driveway for the hard-copy news. Downed four legal-sized cups, made four more.

Was nuking the cream and sugar and the edge of an eye caught the urgent beck of my Clinton era answering machine blinking its ass off.

Hmm. But not that curious yet.

Did another mug of mud, took a decent shit, pushed a button on the machine.

First up was mechanical-me telling you how you should leave a message and I'd call back. Didn't sound too sincere mechanically either.

Next was Ren. Panicked but holding it together. "Great. I called your fucking house, didn't I? Oh well, doesn't matter. He's got me, Sloan. I was watching out the window and one of them just walked up behind Nate and shot him in the head." Noise. "Ah shit, they're kicking the door in." He laughs. "The wall's canvas, the dumb fucks could walk right through it with a pen knife." More banging. "I think your clever little mink may have figured it out, figured the code to the cash. See if you can beat her to it. Here, Sloan." He ran out a mouthful of digits and letters. Finished with, "PIN: small *p,* big *H,* your birthday. Merry Christmas, bitch. I love you. This looks like the big goodbye, so bye." Shouting. A shot. The phone gets dropped. Someone picks it up, uses unknown tongue and it's lights out.

My machine clicked a few times, told me I was outta messages so I threw my coffee mug through the TV screen.

[32]

The smartest person I know is a cupcake with a leche nut on top named Sarah Lee. I once foolishly suggested she try the shamus game.

Not many years back, blaming me, she tried her hand at it. Started in a nice corner unit in a five unit strip. Now she occupied, and owned, the strip. Had operatives and such I suspected. I avoided the place—sounded much like a place I'd bailed on way back.

We still saw each other on a baser level in spite of the staggering difference in our IQ's. I'd call, as well, if I needed some deep work. Always on the gratis because the cupcake felt obligated.

Personally, I felt I'd put a curse on her setting her to the game, but she hadn't gotten there yet. But none of that stopped me from calling for sex and info—sue my lowbrow ass you can find someone clever enough to serve me.

I called. Got a recording but hit *zero* before I became entranced and followed instruction.

"Lee Legal and Discreet. How may I direct your call?" A receptionist I knew.

"Hey, Diana. Tell Cupcake it's Sloan."

Stall to adjust. "Okay. How are you, sir?"

"I got any better, some rich guy'd steal my organs, leave me in a bathtub fulla ice, sweetheart."

Giggles. "Hold please." Click and click.

Click, and, "*Sloan.*" Admonishing, an octave or two higher than the usual subtle purr.

I said, "What?" Like I was simple.

"I wish you wouldn't call me *Cupcake* in front of the help."

We laughed. I said, "Got a pencil ready?"

"Sure. What am I penciling?"

"Don't know, babydoll. Ready?"

"Shoot."

I shot.

Sarah said, "It's an account number, I'd say."

"Yeah?"

"What's up?"

"If it's cash, I want you to see someone gets it. The cop Booker. Tell him it's for Janie Wall's boys. You'll need these numbers to access it: little p, big H..." I fired off the digits to my birthday.

Some quiet tinkering behind the scenes. "And where're you gonna be?"

"With you tonight if you're not busy."

More quiet sounds of thought. "I've got a date."

"Oh. Sorry. Sure."

"Fuck you, Sloan. I don't have a date. I hate you, you bastard. I just..." A nice soft exhale. "Six. And we fuck before we eat."

Last time we were out, we ate, I get a call, I'm gone, so sorry.

The poor child needed reassuring. "I'm gonna bone you till you call your mama, make her come over and beg me to stop."

"She's in Vietnam right now, but don't let that hinder you."

A weaker prick would have told her he loved her. I told her: "No problem. See you at six."

Offed the phone.

Dialed, clued Raleigh.

"So you and Boris going to the dance together?"

"Seems like."

"I don't wanna be an asshole, or seem like I ain't pulling for you, bread, but you think we could square up before you get started on your man Boris?"

"Fuck you. I die, you can go to hell for money."

"You got two thousand dollars' worth of handgun belongs to me too, three grand you consider the trigger lock and signet ring. And that's beyond the extra we bartered on."

Bartered? Nice word for what Raleigh does to my net worth when we play. "Okay, Raleigh, best I got for you: I don't make it, go see Dragonovitch, tell him it was you didn't kill his grandbaby, see if he'll give you a hunk a cheese."

Dropped him. But I'd heard him. The message: *watch your ass.* Come on—you don't pass someone a man-killer and maintain any sort of great expectations. If I failed, then Boris owned what was in my pockets. I prevailed... well then Raleigh owned a gun had popped a fool. Raleigh wasn't looking to get the piece back; he was just trying to be a friend in his fucked up way.

Fired the phone up, punched up some Booker, bad as I didn't want to.

"Mr. Sloan. How we doin? You bust a dozen yet?"

"Probably. I think my friend Alvarez is dead."

Some cop quiet. "Why you think that?"

"Saw some video, got a phone message from him as it went down. I haven't found his skin and bones yet."

"Who was it tagged him?"

"You wouldn't fucking believe it if I told."

"Bet I would. Go ahead on, try me. And tell me bout a video—I like video. Who was it killin your friend?"

Call waiting tinkled. I looked: Cupcake. Shit. "An Eastern-European government-issue cop."

"Hmm. That why Raleigh shot the old dragon's grandboy in the belly?"

Fuck. He knows all, he sees all. "Where'd you hear some shit like that?" Up high, feigning incredulous for his entertainment.

"From a old man work in Ace Hardware." Booker snickered. "Sloan, I'm all over your ass on this thing."

"Makes me wonder why I'm burning cell minutes to clue you then. Call you when I'm done."

Fuck. He was going crazy as I shut him down. He'd be heading my way about right now to talk about it in person.

Gotta move now, Sloan—party time anyway and your bag's still packed and in the car.

And I'm gone as Deadbone and Vaughn Bodé.

★★★

When I had some asphalt under my wheels, I rang Sarah, did the secret handshake.

She came out pushing. "Do you know what this is?"

My mouth opened to defend my ignorance. Didn't make it to a single word.

"The hell's going on? Four-point-seven? And you're passing the PIN around like it was a pre-paid credit card from a gas station."

My mouth got ready to say *wow*. Didn't make it.

"The hell's going on, Duncan?"

Uh-oh: *Duncan*? I didn't even encourage my lips to try it.

"It was five-point-eight, but some shylocks out of Brussels used the difference to lift a Belarusian government hold on it."

Quiet on the Cupcake's end, but I don't got the mox to try it.

Then: "What-the-hell-is-going-on?" Tight jawed now.

"See you at six?"

"Duncan, you hang up on me, I swear I'll shoot you on sight next I see you." Then I got cursed out in some words she'd heard at home growing up.

I was quiet until she said, "Tell me you're still there."

"I'm here. Look, Cupcake, there's this bad guy. He's killed or caused a dozen now. I suspect he's traveling under diplomatic paper."

I pulled over, afraid I was gonna break the steering wheel with my free hand.

"I'm pretty sure he and his..." Man, I'd never even really said it. "...whore stole a few mil from my old friend Rennie and killed him."

I twisted the Vette's key; she shuddered down.

We sat.

We sat.

Then, "What's his name?"

"Boris."

"Boris what?"

I hesitated—paid for it.

"You don't even know, do you? You're going to kill a man and you don't even know his name."

"Does it matter?"

"No, I guess it doesn't. You are going to kill him, right?"

"Sarah, please." I can't say shit. I can't even say, *you don't wanna know.* Couldn't say, *don't ask.*

"*Sarah, please.*" Mocking. "*It's what I do. I'm Sloan, The Great Avenger. I stalk you, I catch you, I try you, I judge you, I sentence you, I even execute the sentence when I can justify it.* Wow, Sloan, God must love you, all the time you save him minding his business."

"No, Sarah, God hates me."

"No, you fuckhead. God loves you—you're still alive. *I* fucking hate you, Sloan. Don't ever call me again."

Poof, and it's gone-daddy-gone, just like that.

[33]

I sat there in the break-down lane watching our inconstant sun bully the environment for a long while. Long enough I began to feel sweat trickle down my chest.

I had nothing. Nothing but a desire to kill Boris's ass. No next step, no next move. With Ren gone and Boris and Iveta totally hostile, I was cauterized. I was dead in the water.

But I live so clean, fate always helps me out. My little buddy from the fernery, Tex, called. He had something to show me. Could I drift his way? Of course I could. What else did I have to do?

***

Tex, bless his little rawhide soul, still toiled among the low shrubs. The brown children still played with gray Florida dirt. Fat Mexican women still smiled corn-ground teeth at me from low concrete porches. My friends, the paranoid live oaks, still squatted nervously in the yard, cringing away from the fickle Florida sky.

Tex saw me, de-stooped and began wiping calloused palms on experienced dungarees. He pulled a brilliantly white handkerchief, mopped then smiled almost apologetically. I wasn't sure I liked the smile.

"How're you, sir?"

I turned and gandered behind me theatrically. "Damn, Tex, all these *sirs*, I thought a cop had snuck up behind me. You need to drop the *sirs* and the *misters.* We've been friends too long for that. You deliver that telegram?" Meaning did he get rid of the gunsel's body.

"Oh, yeah."

"County dumpster?"

"Double bagged."

"Bless you. You said something about a closet in the lab when you called."

"Lemme clean the claws. My daughter and I were straightening up the lab and found something I think you'll wanna see." A hard pause, then, "And I found something else you may not wanna see."

I gave the Mexican kids ones and fives till Tex was decent. He came over, told the oldest kid to go get his mom. The kid answered in Spanglish; Tex grew some grandpa eyebrows, furrowed and unapproving, said, "In English, Albertico. Always in English."

The kid said, "Yessir, grandpa," and took off for the big house.

I smiled and it prompted Tex to say: "They're Americans and they'll act like it in front of me, by God." Little hesitant pause. "Deacon, my daughter found another video on Mr. Alvarez' computer. I'm sorry, but it's some rough shit—prepare yourself."

"Tell me about it, Tex."

He stood his ground. "Come on, see for yourself. It's still got my daughter tore up. I hope she'll come over and run the computer for you."

We walked and I wondered where the dread I should be feeling was. I felt less than nothing. I was numb and empty. I changed subjects.

"Tex, how long you gonna hang?"

He shrugged stoop-labor shoulders. "I know the routes, my daughter runs the office—the legit office." More shrug. "We could pull it off for a bit. The woman gonna be part of the scenery?"

"Mrs. Alvarez? No."

"You know that or guessing?"

"You've met her and her brother. They seem like folks wouldn't mind some honest work?"

"No, I don't think so. You see what I've got for you, you'll see why I'm asking."

"I can assure you, Tex, she's outta the bigger picture."

He wagged his head, said, "That's what you think. Come on. I'll show *you* the big picture."

We walked on quietly and he asked, "If no one's left, what happens now?"

"Rave on. You need a reference, a legal signature, some notary work, a royal seal in wax, whatever it takes to keep the place working, you lemme know—I gotta friend."

"Thank you, pardner. I got seven families relying on this place, all of 'em legal."

"Bullshit."

"*Most* of 'em legal."

We both laughed and I told him he needed good paperwork of that vein as well, my friend specialized in the good, quality stuff.

"He expensive?"

"Of course he is, Tex. How else's he gonna keep out the riffraff?"

"Wouldn't mind getting his number, you don't mind."

"Don't mind at all."

The tool rack was pretty much debris now, its pieces stacked beside the opening it once hid. The tall wooden stool Nate had used lay on its side on top of the pile. Tex and I entered on a clean, orderliness I wouldn't have imagined.

"You guys did clean up in here, Tex."

"Yeah, it was a mess. Mr. Alvarez wouldn't let nobody touch shit in here. And he didn't do clean-up his-own-self."

Too busy being the fool. "Yeah, I noticed. Where's this closet I've heard about?"

"Wait a minute and let's see if Maria'll come over."

Didn't need much more than the minute: a woman with red eyes who was the spitting image of Tex, but in girl and in chubby, stuck her head in demurely.

"Daddy, I can't do this. I can't watch that again."

"S'alright, Maria—I cain't neither. Just set it up and show Mr. Sloan how to start it." Tex made the obvious formal: "Mr. Sloan, this's my daughter, Maria."

I nodded, spoke some civility.

She said, "You were Mr. Alvarez's friend, weren't you?"

I said *yes* and she began to cry softly, but trying to get a handle on it.

She came in, hands partially concealing her face, went by Tex and me to a narrow door. She opened it like there might be werewolves in there, saw none and disappeared into the closet.

Tex watched her go, shook his head empathetically. "Deacon, I found something else this morning too. Somebody's fresh-dug up a patch out beyond the greenhouses. I took the backhoe and dug around some." Pause. "Found a big blue drum."

"You open it?"

"Un-un. Ain't my place to open it, Deacon. It's yours. I'm sorry as hell bout everything."

Maria exited, said, "It's ready. Hit enter on the keyboard. You can pause, fast-forward or reverse with the mouse. Just click at the bottom." She stopped talking, looked at me like I was about to be wrongfully hanged or something. She said, "Mr. Sloan, I am so..." and cried again.

I said, "Thanks, Maria. I got it from here. You can leave. You too, Tex. Like you said: it's my place now. Thanks."

"You gonna let me know what happens?"

"If I'm able. I know you like it American, but *via con Dios*, Tex."

"Same, Deacon. Best of luck."

He put out a sincere, calloused hand. I took it, shook it, and he left me to my toil and trouble.

I pushed my head in the closet. It was a closet-become-office. A tiny metal desk, an uncomfortable metal chair, a tall thin file cabinet, a swing-arm lamp attached to a wall.

Went in, sat in the hard chair, pushed enter. Watched an interior version of the thing Raleigh and I had viewed last night.

This version, dated yesterday, had audio and began with the sound track I'd gotten from Ren when he messaged me, even saw and heard him messaging me. I moused up the volume, leaned into the noise. Looked good up to the part where Rennie would die—a real medicine show.

The view was from a single camera and I couldn't see the door come down, but I heard it. Then Boris and his semi-post-juvenile-delinquent crew showed in frame. Boris goes in a pocket, comes up with a fistful of blue-steel, points it at Rennie's face. Rennie's face does nothing, his eyes widen. My heart jumped up to my collarbone, I pulled in air, watched Boris fire into the ceiling. Rennie jumped, dropped the phone and it hit the table. Boris took the phone from the table where the stunned Rennie had dropped it, spoke the gibberish I'd heard on Ren's message. He glanced at the phone, pushed a button, handed it back to the recovering Rennie.

Rennie looked at the phone like he'd never seen it before, looked at Boris. Said: "The fuck's wrong with you, pointing that thing at me?"

Boris enjoyed it a bit, said, "Just—how do you say it?—keeping it real, friend."

Rennie shook his head, said, "And what the fuck did you shoot the black kid for?"

Boris shrugged. Nothing but a *swarte* in his booklet. "As I said: we have to make it look authentic, Renaldo." More shrugging. "You said he was too friendly with this friend of yours. I do not trust him, you do not trust him. He needed to go. He was only an employee, my employee—why should you care?"

What's Rennie gonna do? He says, "No more. No one else dies."

Boris flapped a hand at Rennie's foolishness, turned and watched his crew roll the empty barrel in. The boys treated themselves to a much deserved smoke break, dropped a couple of bags of soil mix in, recapped it, looked at Boris. He said, "Wait for a minute." Then to Rennie, "I will erase the security video and leave the backup files for your friend." He paused, pinched his lip between a couple of opposing fingers, asked, "You are sure this man Sloan will get these videos to the police?"

Rennie stuck up for my dependable ass: "Absolutely. Sloan's a lot steadier than he appears."

Boris had met me—he wasn't convinced. "He certainly does not look like someone who would possess such a relationship with the authorities."

"He's not you or me, Boris. Sloan's got juice—even with the cops. Don't sweat Sloan, he'll come through. He always does." Rennie shook himself a fistful of pills from his vial while Boris watched through sly eyes. Ren said, "He says you sent the guys who were shooting at me. Did you?"

Look at Rennie riding on nerves of Big Pharma. Good shot, too—it made Boris think.

"Renaldo." A kinder Boris. "Listen to me. Why would I kill you? I am your partner. Yes, I send these people, but these..." Loss for words "...punks, these idiots, have big ideas. I send them to deal with this greedy parole man you foolishly took into your confidence."

"Had to, Boris. I'd have never passed a drug screening."

"Then you should have paid him for the piss and stopped there. But, no, you have to bring him into your business, *our* business. There was no option on his life."

"But they were shooting at me too. I was there, I saw it all."

"This is the *big ideas* I spoke of. I tell these idiots: go destroy the grow houses, scare the people away so we can make it look like you once again have a drug war between you and the blacks. When you disappeared, the authorities were to find out you were killed in this war. It was a good plan, Renaldo. But these punks think they will kill you and then kill me and the grow house business is theirs, all set and ready. So..." His hands came out to corroborate his sincerity. "...they shoot at you and ruin our plan. But forget them. I have dealt with that problem. But now you bring in this Sloan. Why do you do these things, Renaldo, without talking to me first?"

"Because I had a dead woman in one of my grow houses and you weren't anywhere to be found. And maybe I don't trust you so much, Boris."

Boris found that amusing. "*Trust* me? You have no choice, my friend. We are bound together until these IRS problems are solved." Hands out, he says, "Don't I give you what you want most, this facility in Canada? Your dream, Renaldo, remember? And you don't trust me. All these things I do for you, all these plans I make for you."

"We need another plan—I don't like using Sloan like this."

"No. Is a good plan now. You bring in a problem and I make him part of the plan. He dislikes me, so it will be easy to convince him that I am the bad guy, and because of my diplomatic papers, the authorities can not touch me. Is a better plan. You should worry about other things. This is my portion of our deal. Go back to your plants."

Rennie watched Boris, asked: "Why'd you kill the Wall woman?"

Another nice one, Ren. Stalled Boris nicely again.

Boris gathered it up, smiled, leaned on the stainless table across from Rennie, his face a foot and a half from Rennie's. "The woman knew one of the people I sent to break her place. She knew the big red-head white kid, Derrick. She have a big mouth, tell Derrick she will tell you, she will tell the police or he gives her money. So, yes, I go to see her. She puts on her big mouth and I shoot her in the face two times." Boris paused to smile, said, "And I shoot her with the old Walther pistol you are so proud of, the one you have from your father. See, Renaldo? No matter where you turn, I am in front of you. Cooperate, live, go make your millions in Canada."

"I'm not going to put up with it, fuck the Walther. You've gone too far, Boris. They find out all the people you've killed, they'll lock you up for a million years, diplomatic paper or not."

"Who else knows besides you, Renaldo? Iveta?" A laugh. "Remember that she belongs to me. I would advise you not to push your luck."

Rennie says: "I think I already did—and lost." Loud exhale. "I'm fine, Boris. Let's finish it up, okay? Sloan could be here any second."

"No. Your lovely wife is entertaining your old friend. I'm sure, with her talents, he will be busy for some while. You should have an hour or so to pack and get to the airport."

Rennie said, "Sure," conceded the field, went to his stainless steel table and began tinkering. Boris watched him, the doubt obvious.

Rennie goes: "What?"

"You worry me, Renaldo. You have no nerve. Your friend Sloan worries me because he has too much."

"I'm fine. Just stop killing people, Boris. And stop worrying about Sloan. He's steady as a rock."

Boris gave Rennie some more skeptical face. "I hope you are right. Do not lose your spine, farmer." And did a nice exit.

Rennie held up a middle finger at Boris's back and the gun-toters humped the barrel out.

The curtain came down—show over, charade complete.

Not bad but why? Why me? Who was I?

Next thought: if Rennie was vertical, why was I looking at this video? Why wouldn't he take it to where-the-hell-ever he was going? Surely he was going— why else fake your demise?

Again: *Why me?* Why show me shit? Who the fuck was I to vouch for your ass? I wouldn't choose me to vouch for a fucking thing.

Certainly didn't seem like anything to get shook over like Maria and Tex were. *Terrible shit?* I'd been done much worse many times. I mean, what's a little lying, deceit and treachery among old friends? Only one way to go and that was forward. So I fast forwarded to the second feature; it opened on Ren still alive for all appearances, still in lab coat and those stupid plastic shower clogs that people wear out now. He puttered, only clinking sounds on the audio so I moused it down. Ah, he's packing up.

The door opened and the blonde mink slinked in, looking like the millions she'd steal from Rennie. I grew the audio.

No greeting. She poked a phone at Rennie. "Here. You left your phone at home again. The accountant in Vancouver needs you to call."

She's nined out. White long-sleeved blouse, frills spilling down the front. Riding breeches about the color of honey. Nice black boots to knee caps. Kid gloves, black to match the boots, and a simple black bag slung over a shoulder, couple of C's worth of plain black designer shades. I couldn't see the eye but I knew it was black too.

She moved around Rennie, removing her right glove.

Rennie said, "Yeah, I gotta break loose and call some people. I'm calling Sloan, let him know what's going on. He'll play along."

"No. No you will not call him"

"I can't do this to him."

"He can go to hell. We must disappear, Rennie. The tax people are not going to let you go that easy. You know. You have seen the documents. You become someone else—you are a new person now, a Canadian. Tell your friend after a year or two, after the IRS has forgotten you."

Rennie found his pill vial, choked a couple down dry. Then he put the smug face—the one he'd shown me before—on Iveta. "Too late, dear. I gave Sloan the account numbers already."

Iveta whirled back into view, her face contorted but still beautiful. She said, "You did what?"

"The ruse we were pulling on him? I was supposed to call him, right? Well, I called. And I gave him the numbers. I even gave him the password that you and Boris want so badly. See, you two are fucked." He gave her a bland smile—I could assume it being as close as Ren could come to an end-zone dance. "Go take it from Sloan, you want it so badly."

Iveta regrouped, got a grip on her face. "Tell me, why do you do this? Why do you give this insolent bastard these numbers?"

"Insurance—a double-header. Sloan lives like a Franciscan monk. He couldn't spend that much money if he lived five of his lifetimes."

"What is the other part of this double head you have."

Ren smiled, but the pills were drawing a bead on him, about to put him on the mat. "Let me put it like this: now that Sloan's got the money, you and Boris don't really need to kill me, do you? And like I say, dear wife, you and Boris want it so badly, go take it from Sloan."

Iveta said, "So now we only have control of the money in Canada."

"Not we. I called my lawyer..."

Iveta went terminal. "You did what? Call a lawyer? You are supposed to be dead, you fool. Why do you call this lawyer?"

"Don't worry about my lawyer—he knows what I do and he's sitting on a hundred-thousand-dollar retainer—he's cool and quiet."

"Why do you call?" She's well beyond pissed.

"He's gonna take care of a nagging problem—my stealth net worth." Rennie grinned like a loon. "It's being moved over to Sloan's name Monday morning. Done deal." More grin. "You're fucked, Iveta."

Iveta stood totally stunned for a bit. Then she's got: "You are throwing me out with nothing?" Actually sounding like the injured wife.

Ren shrugged, he was slipping off. "You can live at the house, drive the cars until the IRS seizes them. I wish you'd leave now."

Rennie put the beaker he held in his hand in a box, sat on his tall stool. He did his deflating thing. He was done.

Iveta watched from slightly behind Rennie and over his shoulder. She said, "You have become more of a fool than I thought possible, even for you."

Rennie was beat-up, outta game so Iveta found a small pearl-handled auto and shot him in the left ear. He never saw it coming.

The bitch—get this—shucks the left glove, lights a cigarette.

And what am I thinking? I'm thinking*: I didn't know she was left-handed.*

***

Iveta finished her cigarette and watched Rennie. She ground it out on the floor, found her cell and spoke in her tongue to someone. The exchange grew serious legs for a bit until Iveta hung up angrily. One last sneer at dead Rennie, she made her exit.

I got the fast-forward going again, zipped up to an hour or so later and viewed a little more.

Watched enough to catch the stagehands—Doo-Rag and Derrick the White-Boy clean up while Demetree's grandson supervised and smoked cigarettes. Same blue plastic drum, same red hand truck. This time Rennie got to ride in the bucket for real. I killed the video.

Wasn't much to say so I stared at the blank screen, said, "Ah, Rennie, didn't you know you weren't nimble enough to play both ends against the middle with murderers? You were around I'd tell you how I told you so." Sat. Stared. Noodled.

Thanks, Rennie, even if you did use me for my tough-guy attributes. You stuck by me in the end anyway, brother. That was comforting, but cold comfort and outmanned and outgunned by the aftershocks. I clouded over, pondered, concluded: I didn't need fingers anymore to count off the connections to my past. I had no past now. Iveta had casually severed my past, lit her cigarette and walked away.

Dialed the dragon. Got his man. Said: "It's Sloan. Tell Dragonovitch I'm in." Dropped him.

I doused the lights and the computer. Being part caveman, I had no idea how to transport the video, so I unplugged the whole machine, walked it to my car.

Stood there, prepped, walked back to the lower forty.

An old Case backhoe stood at the fence line, a dirty blue drum keeping it company.

I tilted the drum. Its weight was considerable but I could tip it. Removed the clamps and popped the top. The smell was overwhelming: chemically pungent.

Took a few deep ones, cautiously tipped the drum, stepped back quickly. The caustic liquid poured out, fizzled where it contacted organic matter. At the end, a gray blob of slim oozed out, settled on the dirt.

A few things that could have been bone fragments, a few discs of smooth metal I assumed were once coins, but otherwise unrecognizable goo. The ooze settled and I saw the vial, the glass gnome. Then the little plastic St. Christopher Rennie always wore, the ones we'd gotten for our first communion. Oh, Rennie.

I vomited some, then fished the little icon out of the slime with a stick.

[34]

Rennie's St. Christopher washed off and hanging from my rearview by a bit of wire I'd found, I'm rolling. Don't know where, but I'm rolling. Come on, Lady Luck, you hideous bitch, get busy. I'm feeling worthy and I'm wasting gas here.

I ride out a few gallons, circling, so full of juice I could bite myself.

My cell does stuff: Booker. No thanks, not now, Booker.

I ride. More cell: Cupcake. Probably wants to remind me how unconventional I can be at times. Later, Cakes, got some being pissed to deal with right now.

More cell action. Goddamn people. Sneak a peek. Shit: Trevor burning minutes on his new satellite locater.

"Hey, Trev. What's cooking?"

"Just calling." No more.

Fuck it. He had a right to know. "I got him Trevor. I know for sure now."

"Who was it?"

"A secret policeman from Eastern Europe, believe it or not."

"Wow. Why?"

Jeez. Oh, not for much, Trev. She knew a guy who knew a guy. "He's just a bad person. Trevor."

"What'll happen to him?"

"I'll take care of him."

"Cool. Gotta new ring tone. Listen."

I heard Parachute Woman over the tiny speaker. It made me smile a little. I said, "Very cool. Gotta run, kid."

"Alright. Can I still call? I mean, after you take care of this guy?"

"Absolutely. Anytime. We'll talk soon. See you."

The call de-revved me some and I slowed down to a bit faster than reckless but slower than raging. I stopped at a small roadside store, got a tall canned beer and drank it leaning against my car out in the dirt parking lot. I belched and tossed the can, got in, drove on—to nowhere in particular.

More cellular nonsense? That's more like it: the dragon's right-hand calling back. He says some stuff about how word has it a certain fellow happened to be at a certain club as we spoke. Mr. Dragonovitch wondered would I mind running by.

I told the caller I'd be there just about as soon as I was able. He told me Mr. Dragonovitch wished me luck and I thanked him, told him to thank Mr. Dragonovitch and tell him we were right about those three young men.

Pointed myself toward Boris and tried thinking of nothing. Couldn't do it. The two videos kept replaying up there in my balcony section. I kept seeing the gray-green blob that Rennie had become. I couldn't quit glancing at the two-dollar St. Chris. Couldn't quit hearing Boris telling Rennie about shooting Janie Wall in the face twice with Rennie's dad's P-38. I was fucked—nothing worked. I was on a runaway train. Hell, I *was* the runaway train.

Maybe there was enough of Rennie left for DNA. Sure, the nice pictures on the computer in my passenger seat would help the DA build his case. But if Boris and Iveta stayed on script, didn't sell the other out to the cops, there was good chance they'd walk. Fuck, now I knew for fact Boris was traveling under diplomatic paper. Maybe Iveta too. Didn't matter to her. If Boris took a diplomatic pass, she'd just play it out as the innocent, slighted wife. Maybe the DA would luck out, get a blind judge who couldn't be swayed by that enchanting face of Iveta's.

Maybe, maybe, maybe.

Damn sorry, but not good enough.

I put my mind a million miles from nowhere, fired the booster rockets, locked in the radar.

Yep, all over but the shouting now.

***

Put the Shark on the street side of Boris's borrowed Escalade. I bellows-ed my lungs a bit, stuck a hand in my pocket and jingled the Wall boys' fifty-six cents. I watched the Bohunk clubhouse door a few beats, said fuck it, made my move.

I'm on the asphalt, head down, casual left hand goes under my over-shirt, brushes my Smith for reassurance, right drifts back in position, palm-assward in my hip pocket.

I'm on the concrete walkway. I close my eyes to the daylight, anticipating a darker atmosphere inside. I pulled the door left-handed, not sure it would cooperate. Oh my, someone's expecting me: the door surrendered quietly.

If I was looking for casbah, I didn't get it. I was stunned by the simplicity of the room. Yeah, there was some damned nice tile-work on the floor, but no draped walls or dancing girls. Not a hookah in sight, but it was dark as private sin inside.

More like a small retail space converted to a private bar, which I guess it was. A few small tables on each side, a long simple melamine counter served as a bar across most of the back end. The short, round fellow who'd answered the knock my first visit was behind the bar. He wore either a similar or same short-sleeved white shirt.

Dragonovitch was with peers at the bar, all holding big-ass shot glasses. He and his peeps froze, mid-toast, checked my shit.

Boris sat first table on the right. He was doing what seemed to be one of those number puzzles, an early cocktail on his flattop.

He looks up, sees me in the failing glow of the closing door. Does well with it, the prick.

He says, “The fuck you come to my place for? The hell are you, come here, disrespect me and my people? Get the fuck out.”

I pulled the Smith and did him three solids in the chest. Didn't worry much about pretty but they ended up in a decent pattern. He went over, face into his Sudoku. His feet buffed the tile some, scuffing his loafers on the table's stand.

I scoped the bar, said, “Anybody want a piece of this? Anybody gonna feel the need to see me about this later needs to say it now.” I let Messrs. Smith and Wesson's best hang, not wanting to be viewed as a kook and a pistol-waver or something. “Anybody looking to buy in?”

No one had shit. Boris moaned.

I stepped over, eyes still all over the six, eight guys at the bar, flipped the table cloth over Boris's head. Laid the Nine against his skull and did him up. He kicked out and I began backing out of the place.

Demetree the ice cream eater grins paternally, says, “Even.”

I go, “Even, Papa.” Put up a frail smile but still backed the fuck out.

One down, one to go and I'd have myself a Booker's dozen—an even fourteen.

[35]

Dead Rennie's gates were still on his luscious lawn. A car, not the Mercedes but some other sort of European tragedy, sat alone on the pink pavers. A couple of good sized travel bags waited patiently at the opened trunk. The now-plywooded previously-glass door that some outrageous asshole had once gone through stood ajar.

I planted the Shark next to the Teut-mobile, sat there watching nothing. I wondered if I sat long enough, could I shrug it all off, drive away a bigger and better man.

The fuck was I kidding? I was no more prone to change than the four points on the compass. And what I was at that minute was as ancient as those four winds.

I was the crocodile, submerged but for eyes. I was the coiled snake. The cocked fist. I was all and more—I wasn't driving off.

I grabbed the piece Raleigh had lent me, dug around in my back storage and found an old Stiff Records tee that told you what it was if it wasn't Stiff. I nestled the gun in the shirt and used Rennie's pavers one more time. Why knock?

Cruised in, stopped in the foyer. Mouse sounds upstairs but no gunsels about anymore. Must be close to curtain time. Or simply no one much left alive of the major cast.

Half-way up the stair, I unraveled Raleigh's gat, checked the chamber, checked the safety, massaged the magic signet ring on my finger.

Turned left, stood in the doorway to Iveta's bedroom. I could hear her moving about efficiently in the closet.

She exited, flapped a silky sweater, folded it over twice and saw me. So, so cool—damn near no reaction. These people, it seemed, had nerves of titanium.

In a nice move, Iveta turned and stepped between me and a tall blonde wardrobe. Wasted effort—I'd already seen her little pearl-handled auto laying on a corner of the wardrobe.

She's got: "Well, well. I did not think I would see you again."

"Why?"

She shrugged like Boris did when he was still wasting air. "Rennie left for Canada. He's gone. He said should I see you to tell you..."

"I shot your brother in the head." Got a reaction from that. Then I got skepticism.

"Where?"

"In the Belarusian Club."

More skepticism plus a smile like I was kidding her about something. She started to speak.

I cut her off. "Demetree Dragonovitch sends his regards." I was cruel: I watched her squirm. "He says you and Boris aren't related. He says you're a whore who worked for Boris as a snitch in the old country."

Now I got fear from her face. She took a step back. "Dragonovitch is going to kill me?"

"He says they don't kill women. You believe him?"

"No. Dragonovitch is a murderous bastard. He would kill anyone." Another nonchalant step back.

Enough of that shit. "That little auto laying there, that the one you used on Rennie?" Pointed with my eyes.

My bad: she spun, lunged for the pistol.

I crossed the room in three quick strides, caught her arm as she turned, gat in hand. She got off a wild one before I trapped her between my body and the wardrobe. I banged the pretty hand full of Lady Smith against the wardrobe hard enough to disarm her, stepped away to watch.

This go, I got hate. The hate was as old and deep and seething as my crocodile eyes.

Her words were spat at me, her English failing her. "You are big me, yes? Big, big man. So you push women. What if I are man?"

"I'd a shot you in the back a the head when you went for the gun if you were a man."

Different tact: "How do you like fucking with a whore?"

I gave her back one of the family shrugs. "I've fucked worse than whores before. Hell, I've been a whore before. What else you got?"

New face: slow terror. "For what? For you to not kill me?"

I realized how tired I was. Bone tired, dead weary. Fed up, over it, whatever the fuck it was. I looked at the fancy gat in my hand, back to Iveta.

She said, "Fuck me."

"No, dollbaby. We're past all that."

"Duncan, please." The kitten now. "How much Dragonovitch offer you? We can buy Demetree Dragonovitch now, if you have killed Boris for sure." She slinked toward me, hips forward, leading the way for the queen's gambit. "Three million in cash and stocks legal, in Canada bank. Maybe another two million in the facility there." Nice smile as she slinked. "We are rich."

"What about the big cache Boris had his eye on? You know, that annoying six mil he'd locked down and needed Rennie to retrieve for him."

"There is that also. And the real estate here, the art, boats, a small plane." She was on me, arms wrapping me up, sliding hands over me in practiced moves. "Go with me."

"You shot my friend."

"He was not a friend. He speaks badly of you. He wished to use you." Sincere, melting into my eyes. "Duncan, I am not a killer. Boris is the killer. He killed Renaldo, not me. I could no more kill him than I could kill you. Only you scare me, how you look at my eyes."

Here it comes—the kiss of death.

She reached up on tip-toes for my smiling lips, her arms reaching around me.

I wasn't expecting the knee to the jewels, but I knew she wanted the piece in my hand. I let her have it, bent a bit, shaking off the knee slam.

She had the big gat up, pointing it at me. "So, how are you liking it now, you ass?"

I liked it fine except for being nut-racked, but that too would pass. "You need to do the safety if you're gonna shoot me."

Smart girl: she backed away from me, looked at the gat, flipped the safety, "You are also a stupid ass. Now I shoot *you.*"

I tossed out such a casual, *okay*, she shoulda been suspicious. Maybe the hate had her blinded.

She squeezed. Nada, but behind the gigantic bore of Raleigh's piece was a surprised face. She tried several more times, the gun quivering from her efforts to pull the trigger.

I asked, "Did you get the safety right?"

She actually looked. She also was trained enough to ease the slide back, see the shell in the breech. Everything seemed in order, so she tried to shoot me four or five more times.

The shock wore off and she tossed the gun at me, dove for her Lady Smith still idling on the carpet. I was once again faster, stepped on the gun, grabbed her by the silky ashen hair, pulled her away.

She fell against the wardrobe and cursed me in both English and her fist tongue. I retrieved the Lady Smith, cleared it, pocketed the clip and the shell from the chamber, threw it on the bed.

When I turned, Iveta had Raleigh's high-tech shit again, trying to trick it into popping me.

I pulled my Nine from the back of my pants, said, "Bye-bye, babydoll. You're one wicked little bitch."

The juice starts flowing so hard my ears are muffled, my heart has moved up a couple of inches and is beating under my collarbone, my eyes glow. My palms drench up, my lower abdomen and anus buzz.

I can smell me. I can smell Iveta. I can smell the room.

Iveta's begging Russian, crying universal. I can't identify anymore. The part of me running the machinery isn't a stranger but I don't know him. The other part, the better part, turns in disgust, walks away, leaving the crocodile alone with Iveta in the killing pond.

My piece comes up; I kick the safety forward with my thumb. I note how my breathing, though somewhat deep, is metered perfectly. I put my finger on the trigger, slide it back and forth on the smooth cool steel.

The finger slides into position.

Movement in my left peripheral.

Booker said, "Whoa, Sloan," over there somewhere. "Whoa now."

"Stay outta this, Booker." My eyes and iron sights stayed on the bitch.

"Stay out? It's my fuckin job, Sloan. Come on, man."

Iveta says: "Shoot him. Kill him."

"Sloan, take your finger off the trigger, man. For God's sake, don't make me shoot you."

Iveta's over there screaming for my head; no one hears her much.

"She killed my best friend, Booker, then she and the Euro-trash cop dissolved him in a drum fulla some sorta acid. You ever see one a your own dissolved in acid, Booker? Ugly, dad. Smells bad too."

"We got her. You let her go, we'll see her and her partner pays up. I promise, Sloan."

"Please, Booker. Think about who you're talking to. Dumb-fucks walk past justice on a parade basis—these two would slip through like they'd been greased." Still on Iveta, I nodded at her. "They were all playing me, even my friend Rennie for a while, huh, sweetpants? Tell the man about it. How I was supposed to find the security tapes, show everybody how Rennie was brutally murdered by some phantoms who'd vanished."

Iveta had gone quiet.

"Here's the funny part, Booker. My buddy left me a number to an account full of millions thinking I was a monk, would hold his dough, and, get this, I gave it away already."

Iveta's pretty mouth was open.

Booker said, "I heard about it."

Ah. And I thought she hated me. "My friend Sarah Lee called you, huh?"

"That's why I'm here, Sloan. She seemed to think you needed saving from an appointment with the lethal-injector doctor up at Raiford. She said you had four, five million dollars you wanted to see went to the Wall boys."

"Good. I gotta new video for you. One nobody but Rennie knew about." I gestured to the quiet Iveta. "Nice pictures, with audio, of this piece of fluff shooting him in the left ear. Used that Lady Smith lying over there."

Iveta came alive. "Liar. He killed Renaldo and my brother. Killed them for this millions dollars."

No one was hearing her.

Booker goes: "I got your buddy's jacket, Sloan. He wasn't no door prize, sure wasn't worth this. This shit ain't nothin but a territory war tween your man and some East-Europe gangsters. Bout nothin but dope, Sloan. Let it go."

"Bullshit, Booker. It's not about dope—it's never been about the dope. It's about the money. Always the money. Nothing but. Same story here. Her and her pimp smelled money, set my friend up, then she killed him when she found out he was gonna give it all to me."

Iveta insisted it was all a lie but Booker was busy with me. "So what? Was the old badger game. What's it to you whe're it's thugs or drugs?"

"It's the last off my past, dad, all spilled out and fizzling on the ground in a citrus grove. Nah, I'm doing her, Booker."

"No you ain't. Goddam don't make me shoot you, man."

Iveta voted yes loudly on shooting me.

I stayed on her, said, "I don't think you will, Booker. Besides that, wouldn't shooting me be sorta moot after I shoot her?"

Iveta finally agreed with something I'd said. Said, "Yes, yes. Shoot him now."

"Shut up, lady. Sloan, you pop her, I'm poppin you. Swear on it, sure do, swear on it, now. Fuck *moot*, I'll pop you."

"Nah, I don't think so. I'm icing her. You don't wanna watch, you need to go downstairs or something."

"You hearing me? You hear me say I'll shoot your ass?"

"Yeah. I just don't believe it. We share that fucked up sense a justice, remember?"

"Un-huh. But I'm a cop first..."

Iveta got loud again, yelled at Booker that it wasn't a debate. *Shoot him, shoot him.*

"Shut up, lady. I'm tryin to save your miserable life here. Shut up."

She couldn't.

"Sloan..."

"You leaving, Booker?"

"Sloan, you shoot *her*, I shoot *you.*"

"Don't think so, Booker."

And I dropped the hammer.

Somewhere off to my left, last thing I heard was Booker's old revolver discharge.

4639964R00124

Printed in Germany
by Amazon Distribution
GmbH, Leipzig